MARTÍN KOHAN

School for Patriots

Translated from the Spanish by Nick Caistor

A complete catalogue record for this book can be obtained from the
British Library on request

The right of Martín Kohan to be identified as the author of this work
has been asserted by him in accordance with the Copyright, Designs
and Patents Act 1988

First published as *Ciencias Morales* in 2007
by Editorial Anagrama, Barcelona
First published in this English translation in 2012
by Serpent's Tail,
an imprint of Profile Books Ltd
3A Exmouth House
Pine Street
London EC1R 0JH
website: www.serpentstail.com

ISBN 978 1 84668 743 3
eISBN 978 1 84765 645 2

Designed and typeset by Crow Books

Printed by CPI Group (UK) Ltd, Croydon, CR0 4YY

10 9 8 7 6 5 4 3 2 1

School for Patriots

I

In the past, the National School of Buenos Aires was an establishment for boys. In those distant days when it was knowna as the School of Moral Sciences, or in the even more remote era when it was called The Royal College of San Carlos, things must have been more straightforward, more orderly. It's simple: eactly half of the world it now contains weren't there. The half made up of jumpers, hairbands, ribbons and hair-slides, the half that required the installation of separate toilets in the school and separate changing rooms on the playing fields, once, a long time ago, in the days of Miguel Cané, or Amadeo Jacques, simply didn't exist. The school was a single entity, all boys. In those days, all the school activites must have taken place in a much calmer atmosphere. Or at least this is what the class assistant for the third year class ten thinks, as her mind begins to wander near the end of the second afternoon break. Everyone knows her as María Teresa, unaware that in the evenings, at home, she is known as Marita. This is what she, the teaching assistant for the third year class ten, is thinking absentmindedly, although she is apparently paying close attention, when more than eight minutes of the ten-minute break have already gone by. She thinks this without realising that, if the conditions from those days of the school's splendour still applied, she herself would not be able to occupy the position she currently occupies at the school, because just as there had been no girl pupils, there had been no female teachers, and no female assistants. Contrary to the present situation, in those days this world was not split in two: the main aim back then, as can be seen from the school's literary classic called *Juvenilia* (which the current crop of students, out of ignorance or spite, insist on calling 'Juvenilla'), was probably something quite different: to ensure the pacific co-existence of boys from Buenos Aires with those from Argentina's interior provinces. This mix often gave rise to disturbances, even unseemly brawls which ended in cuts and bruises, and yet none of that was anything like what it takes to keep a close eye on this other reality of males and females in close proximity. After all, for boys from Buenos Aires to fight provincials was nothing more than the expression of a deep-seated truth about Argentinian history. It served to demonstrate that the school was already what it had been intended to be: a select microcosm of the entire nation. Had not Bartolomé Mitre, the school's founder, happily defeated Urquiza, from Entre Ríos province, at the battle of Pavón? Had not the federalist tyrant Juan Manuel de Rosas kept the school closed during the dark period of his rule that had afflicted Argentina for so many years? Had not Domingo Sarmiento, born in San Juan province, unsuccessfully tried to enrol at the school? And did not the boy from Tucumán, Juan Bautista Alberdi, succeed where Sarmiento had failed, giving

4

rise to a feeling of resentment that lasted throughout the remainder of Sarmiento's life? The fights between pupils of Buenos Aires and the provinces were part of the school's history because the school itself was part of the nation's history. Miguel Cané writes about this openly in *Juvenilia*. No matter that today's pupils talk about the book as if they had never heard of it; in reality, they have all read it and are well aware of the significant fact that the school made no distinction between students from the northern provinces and those born in Buenos Aires. Ensuring the peaceful co-existence of these two groups was perfectly possible for a master like Amadeo Jacques, who was born in France, or for a Headmaster like Santiago de Estrada. But the school then had been only for boys. María Teresa is merely letting her mind wander rather than making comparisons, but she knows her job as an assistant is very different nowadays. She has no illusions that she can cast herself in the same mould as those illustrious male predecessors; as she stands in the playground gazing blankly around her she simply allows one thought after another to slide by, and in this daydream imagines what the more homogeneous, more harmonious version of the school that existed in the nineteenth century, in another age, must have been like. The sound of the bell, which the others usually calculate precisely, startles her out of her daydream: the end of break. The bell rings – firmly but not stridently – for exactly fifty-five seconds, just short of a minute. Everyone is aware of this. There is a very precise reason why they should know this, and for their timing to be as exact as the sound itself instead of allowing themselves the rough approximation of a minute. That is because the moment the bell stops ringing (and without its echo being considered part of the process), all the pupils must line up, in total silence and in ascending order of height, outside their classroom door.

Third year class ten lines up in front of the penultimate door in the quad. Quite often, footsteps, a shoe scraping against the ground, sometimes even a laugh can be heard after the bell has ceased to ring, and then it is the assistants' job to step in.

—Silence, ladies and gentlemen.

After this warning, there ought to be no noise at all. If the earlier sound was a sign that someone was slow to respond, the assistants have to make sure that following this carelessness the pupils are absolutely quiet. If, on the other hand, there was the more serious offence of a laugh or the suggestion of laughter, they have to try to identify the joker (who in all likelihood would persist in their misdeed), take him or her out of the line, and proceed to punish them. The culprits usually gave themselves away by staring at the ground.

More often than not, however, the order to be silent is strictly obeyed.

—Step apart.

A single voice echoes all round the quad. Because of the height of the roofs or the thickness of the walls, the sound seems to rebound and multiply, but despite this, everyone knows nothing has been repeated, that orders are given only once, and that this is enough.

Stepping apart is a fundamental part of teaching the pupils how to behave properly. Even though they are now in lines, and even though they correctly position themselves from smallest to tallest, until they have stepped apart, the pupils still look disorderly, grouped but not formed up. They look untidy, and that is intolerable. Once they have stepped apart, however, the double line has an orderly, structured appearance, creating an appropriate symmetry. To step apart the pupils must raise their right arms – without of course bending the elbow – and rest their hands (even better if it is just the tips of their fingers) on the right shoulder of the classmate in front. Since by definition this classmate is smaller than the one behind, each arm makes a perfectly straight line but slopes gently downwards. That is how it is and always has been. The girls form up in front, the boys behind. Although she tries to do so discreetly, María Teresa focuses her attention on the most problematic link in the chain, the point where the two smallest boys follow on from the two tallest girls. In general, the smallest boys are those who still look like smooth-cheeked infants, whereas the tallest girls are always the most mature. When instructed to step apart, those two boys (who in third year class ten are Iturriaga and Capelán) have to place their hands – or better still, the tips of their fingers – on the shoulder of the girls in front (in third year class ten that means Daciuk and Marré). The shoulders are quite far away, and are higher than them, so the boys almost have to stretch in order to reach them. María Teresa examines the point of contact closely. Of course, her concern is not the height difference, or that by stretching out their arms Iturriaga or Capelán might lose their posture. It is

MARTÍN KOHAN

not that, nor is it the vigorous gesture their arms make as they straighten and aim upwards. No, it is something else. María Teresa has to pay particular attention to what happens to those boys' hands on each girl's shoulder for as long as this stepping apart lasts – and this is something which, unlike the bell for the end of break, does not go on for a fixed, predetermined length of time, but depends on the personal decision of Señor Biasutto, the supervisor of the team of assistants.

—Stand to attention!

It is only when Señor Biasutto has given this order that the pupils' arms drop and contact between them ceases. By now, all of them are in their rightful place, at the required distance from each other, and they may now be allowed to enter the classroom. And yet it frequently happens that Señor Biasutto delays giving the order and allows the moment of contact to drag on. This may be to make sure that the line for each year is properly formed up, or to give the assistants he is in charge of time to detect any possible irregularity among the pupils. If there is the slightest sign that this delay is making them impatient, Señor Biasutto will not hesitate to prolong it.

—I'm in no hurry, ladies and gentlemen.

On an earlier afternoon, at the end of first break, María Teresa noticed, or thought she noticed, that Capelán's right hand was resting *excessively* on Marré's right shoulder. He had stepped apart from her as required, but perhaps had gone further than that. It was one thing to use her shoulder as a marker to take distance from; it was another altogether to grasp the shoulder, touch it, cup it in the hand, to give Marré a sensation that was neither fleeting nor innocent.

8

—Are you tired, Capelán?

—No, Miss.

—Is your arm heavy, Capelán?

—No, Miss.

—Perhaps you'd like to leave the line-up, Capelán, and have a little rest in Señor Biasutto's office?

—No, Miss.

—Well then, step apart in the proper manner.

—Yes, Miss.

There is nothing suspicious about the way Iturriaga steps apart from Daciuk. Capelán is the one María Teresa needs to pay close attention to. Ever since her warning to him the other afternoon, which only by a miracle did not lead to Señor Biasutto being involved, Capelán has become very subtle; perhaps too subtle, which is also a nuisance. He is no longer touching Marré with the palm of his hand, but with his fingers, which is good; in fact, only with his fingertips, which is better still. He does not even rest those fingers, or the tips of them, on her shoulder: they simply hover, almost without touching, as they might do with a door he had to half-close, or close without a sound. But in that lightest and apparently so circumspect of movements, María Teresa sees, or thinks she can see, that Capelán is caressing rather than touching the girl. Capelán is no longer pressing too heavily on Marré's shoulder, but appears instead to have openly replaced that misdemeanour with another: he is brushing against her. Scarcely touching her, as though he wanted to tickle or startle her.

—What's the matter, Capelán, are you feeling weak?

—No, Miss.

—Then step apart in the proper way.

9

The hovering hand, the aerial, deceptively innocent hand Capelán is stretching out as if thoughtlessly, moves towards Marré's shoulder, towards that reassuring, solid part that follows the curve of the blue school uniform pullover. But because it is a hesitant, vague gesture, suspiciously obedient of the warning not to press down, the hand hangs there and seems to feel rather than touch, to caress almost like a blind person would do, so that before it reaches Marré's shoulder it might (or at least this is the impression María Teresa has) brush against Marré's neck: the sky-blue collar of her school shirt, or worse still, the neck itself, the skin on Marré's neck, in other words, Marré herself.

—Are you feeling ill, Capelán?

—No, Miss.

—Is your hand trembling, Capelán?

—No, Miss.

—Are you sure, Capelán?

—Yes, Miss.

—That's good.

This is the first year, as autumn slowly gives way to winter, that María Teresa has worked as an assistant at the National School of Buenos Aires. She started in February, when the weather was still hot, three weeks before the March exams, and six before the new school year began. She had a first interview with the Head of Discipline, who decided to take her on. This was followed by a fifteen-minute interview with the assistants' supervisor, Señor Biasutto. He informed her, amongst other things, of the best attitude to adopt to keep a close eye on the pupils. It was no easy matter to achieve what Señor Biasutto referred to as 'the ideal stance'. The ideal stance to keep the closest watch. An attentive gaze, taking in every last detail, would mean that no misbehaviour or violation of the rules escaped her. But precisely because she was looking on so attentively, this would serve as a warning to the pupils. The ideal stance required a gaze that surveyed everything, but which itself was able to pass unnoticed. The teachers were well aware of this; that was why, whenever there was a written test, they stood at the back of the classroom, so that they could see without being seen. Any sideways glance inevitably betrayed a pupil attempting to copy from a neighbour. The school assistants had to acquire a similar expertise if they wanted to be as relentlessly alert. Not 'staring into space' as an absent-minded person might do, but seeing everything while giving the impression of not looking at anything.

María Teresa follows this detailed advice from Señor Biasutto at the end of each of the three afternoon breaks: at the moment when the pupils line up, and when they step apart. She uses it to keep an eye on that idle-looking boy Capelán. Apart from Iturriaga, all his classmates are taller than him. That is why he is the first boy in the line. Marré is directly in front of him. He can touch her: it is allowed. More than that: he is obliged to do so. He must put his hand on her shoulder, or better still, place the tips of his fingers on her shoulder, so that he can step apart from her. So María Teresa pretends to be looking at nothing in particular: not looking nowhere, which would be taking things too far, but a look not focused on anything in particular. Of course, in reality she is concentrating on what is going on between Capelán and Marré's shoulder: between Capelán's hand, or fingers, and Marré's shoulder. She is pretending to look all round her, but in fact her eyes are trained on that tiny detail. She wears glasses, and straightens them now. She sees, or thinks she sees,

Capelán moving his fingers slightly. Possibly he has stroked Marré's shoulder. Imperceptibly, María Teresa focuses even more intently to scrutinise the expression on Capelán's face. It looks as innocent as the expression on the face of Iturriaga, who alongside him has stretched out his hand without even appearing to notice how close Daciuk is to him. But María Teresa is well aware that this vague expression proves nothing. The pupils brazenly practise the art of dissembling. She takes a slow, deliberate step forward. Now she is no longer level with Capelán, but with Marré. The face she is secretly studying is Marré's, not Capelán's. She notices, or thinks she notices, a slow closing of Marré's eyes: something akin to a blink, but in slow motion. María Teresa interprets this as she thinks she is meant to interpret it: she sees a gesture of annoyance in this lowering of the eyelids. She cannot be certain, but there is no time for her to wait to be certain that this is what it means.

—Is something wrong, Marré?

—No, Miss.

—Are you sure? I thought it looked as if you felt ill.

—No, Miss.

—Are you sure?

—Yes, Miss.

—Good.

At that moment Señor Biasutto gives the order for them all to stand to attention. The pupils lower their arms and stare at the nape of the neck of the classmate in front of them. Whatever the weather outside, the light in the quad is always that of a cloudy day. The walls are covered halfway up in green tiles: beyond that they are bare. The order is given for the pupils to enter their classrooms.

That night, María Teresa's sleep is strangely disturbed.

Without intending to, she dreams of Marré's face and the fleeting expression she caught there. She remembers almost nothing of her dream apart from that image, but it is very vivid: the face of the girl at school whose name is Marré. She is still in a daze even after she has woken up, made her bed, brushed her teeth, hung her clothes in the wardrobe, kissed the rosary, put her hair up, and opened the curtains. Then she dons a faded housecoat and buttons it all the way up to her neck. She goes into the kitchen, where her mother is waiting for her with breakfast. The radio stands beside the table. The news bulletin is on as they say good morning to each other.

—Did you sleep well?

—Yes.

Her mother does not sit at the table with her. Possibly she has already had breakfast, or does not want any. She is busy boiling something for lunch; the smell is unpleasantly pungent and sweet for this time of morning. The mother watches the water bubble as if there is not enough heat or time for it to come to the boil properly. The two women do not talk: the only voice to be heard is that of the newsreader. Today's news: the skies over Buenos Aires will be cloudy, the lakes in Palermo Park are to be refurbished, there has been a drop in cinema attendance, early snowfalls in Mendoza province, two Dutch scientists have proved that animals dream, the temperature in the capital will not rise above thirteen degrees.

—What's making that smell?

—In the pan, d'you mean?

—Yes.

—Beetroot.

On the radio, the news has given way to adverts. A jingle about wrist watches that keeps ending then suddenly starting up again is followed without a break by an aspirin commercial.

—Don't you like beetroot?

—I don't know.

—What do you mean, 'I don't know'?

—Just that, I don't know.

—Don't start getting fussy, Marita, you've always liked them.

An unopened envelope lies on the table under the vase stuffed with imitation flowers. María Teresa spots it and asks what she already suspects, what in fact she knows deep down: if the letter is from her brother. The mother says it is. And that this time she has decided not to open it because of what always happens whenever she does: as soon as she sees her absent son's handwriting, and even before she starts reading what it says, she bursts into tears. She prefers Marita to read the letter and tell her what is in it.

With two fingers María Teresa tears open a top corner of the envelope. She slides the knife she has not yet used for the butter or cheese into the slit. Her mother does not look at her as she does this. Strictly speaking, it is not a letter, only a postcard. Francisco likes his little jokes. In fact, he is not very far away; he's only in Villa Martelli. If the two women chose to travel to Avenida Pacífico and catch either the number 161 (the red sign) or even better the 67 (any sign), they could be at his regiment's front gate in less than an hour. They do not do so because there would be no point: even if they went there, they would not be allowed to see or wave to Francisco. But he is still quite close, on the outskirts of Buenos Aires. He loves to play the clown, sending them a postcard as if he were a long way off. He must have borrowed or bought it from one of his colleagues from the provinces who collects them to send one by one to his family back home. A lad from the south, or perhaps from Formosa in the north. María Teresa takes the postcard from the envelope. It is of Buenos Aires. An aerial view of the Obelisk in bright sunlight, with dense traffic encircling it on the world's widest avenue. At the edges she can make out a line of not very tall buildings of uneven height.

María Teresa turns the postcard over and discovers that her brother has written only: 'I can't seem to make friends'.

María Teresa glances at the picture a second time: a red bus she did not notice before is driving round the Obelisk. She puts the card back in the envelope and replaces it under the plastic vase. The flowers, also made of plastic, have drooped so far they no longer resemble real flowers at all. María Teresa tries to make them stand upright, but without success: as if they were capable of remembering or having preferences like human beings, the plastic stems flop back to their previous position.

The mother meanwhile has covered the pan on the stove again. She turns and leans against the table edge. She is holding, or rather clutching, a tea towel decorated with red hearts.

—Tell me what your brother says.

María Teresa puts her knife down on the plate, among the breadcrumbs, next to the used teabag.

—Francisco says he is fine. That he misses us, but that he's fine.

2

Better he had died, says her mother, crossing herself because she knows what she is saying is sacrilege. Better for him to have died than to be sent God knows where. At least that way there would have been a piece of paper, some sort of certificate, and that way poor Francisco could have avoided all his suffering from the cold draughts, the unhealthy food served on aluminium plates. For the three or possibly four weeks of his basic training, he is allowed no passes or leave. Only once, at seven in the morning as day is breaking on an as yet undetermined date, will he be given permission to come to the gate on Avenida San Martín to say hello to his family standing outside.

The mother cries at least once a day. Sometimes María Teresa hears her from the bedroom; sometimes, even though she cannot see or hear her, she can sense her mother is in tears. She often cries when she listens to the radio news, when they give the temperature and say that the weather is turning cold: and there is news on the radio every half hour. At first María Teresa would stop whatever she was doing and try to comfort her mother, but she is one of those people who do not want to be comforted and so will not allow it to happen. In the end María Teresa decided to let her cry and unburden herself as much as possible.

Because the pupils who have afternoon school start at ten past one precisely, the teaching assistants have to be there by half-past twelve. Several of them work mornings and afternoons, but not María Teresa. She works afternoons only, and lives half an hour away from the school, provided there are no delays on the metro. So as not to be in a rush, she leaves home at a quarter to twelve. Often her mother is still crying when she goes out.

Occasionally, usually when the Head of Discipline decides he needs to see Señor Biasutto and his team of assistants, her starting time can be an hour or two earlier. Since María Teresa has worked as an assistant, there have been two such meetings. The first was devoted to the problem of the pupils who were in school out of hours. There are some curricular activities, such as using the physics or chemistry labs, or going for swimming lessons in the basement, as well as extra-curricular activities like visiting the library to study, which the pupils need to attend out of their school hours. Yet that is no reason, the Head of Discipline emphasised, fingers raised and the tic in his eyebrows beating furiously, that is no reason for them to be strolling round the corridors or running up and down the staircases without any good reason. The assistants had the authority and, more than that, the obligation, to stop any pupil they saw wandering around the school and demand their identity card, so that they could check the photograph, name, and whether they were enrolled for morning or afternoon sessions, and if an afternoon pupil was in the school during the morning, or a morning pupil was there in the afternoon, they should demand an explanation. After being granted permission by the Head of Discipline, Señor

Biasutto then insisted that only clear, direct explanations should be considered valid. Señor Biasutto is held in high esteem at the school because everyone knows that a few years earlier he had been the person chiefly responsible for drawing up the lists. It is generally expected that at some point, in accordance with the dynamics of administrative appointments, he will one day become Head of Discipline.

The second meeting which meant María Teresa had to come in early to school was called to clarify exactly how far geographically the assistants' authority extended. The school regulations cover not only the interior of the building, as well as the sports facilities which are located in the port area of the city, but stretch to two hundred metres beyond the actual entrance to the institution. This includes the entire block where the school stands, including the part outside San Ignacio church, as well as the next block towards Plaza de Mayo (the block stretching from Calle Alsina to Calle Hipólito Yrigoyen) and the one opposite, which goes from Calle Moreno to Avenida Belgrano: in other words, the whole block mostly occupied by the school buildings, which is widely known as the 'Block of the Enlightenment' in the city's history. All this area is governed by the norms and penalties set out in the school's regulations. In other words, on the street corner or round it, or indeed on the pavement opposite, the assistants are on duty and should pay attention, for example, to whether the boys are wearing their blue ties askew, or have the top button of their shirts undone, whether the girls no longer have their hair in a hairband, or are not fastening their blue blouses with the regulation twin blue ribbons. In addition, the behaviour of all students from the National

School of Buenos Aires should be strictly exemplary at all times and wherever they might be. This means the assistants are required to intervene whenever they detect any misconduct, wherever it may occur, and report it as soon as possible to the school authorities, whether this be the Head of Discipline or Señor Biasutto. An oft-quoted example of this is the case of the fifth year class five pupils punished at the end of the previous school year for having behaved in a very inappropriate manner in Calle Florida, perhaps the busiest street in the city, without realising that a school assistant who happened to be passing by had seen and noted their unruly behaviour.

As someone new to her position, all these requirements have led María Teresa to consider, and indeed to correct, a tendency of hers since childhood (as her mother still reminds her, and as her father never tired of telling her): that of becoming easily distracted, of letting her mind wander far from the matter at hand. Now, however, she is learning to stay alert, and is even trying out different physical or mental techniques to help rid herself of the ingrained habit of allowing her mind to stray. Now she pays attention: as much as she can and for as long as she can. She does this above all at school, in the quad during break-time, and in the classrooms during the few minutes it takes the teachers to arrive once break is over. She also concentrates hard in the street, as the Head of Discipline has urged them to do, on the street corner or in the metro, as well as at the newspaper kiosk and the flower stall near the school.

This is how, as she strolls apparently casually on one of her preventive forays along the pavement where the pupils congregate five minutes before going into school, she suddenly comes across a flagrant example of unacceptable behaviour: she sees Dreiman openly leaning against Baragli. Until that moment everything seemed so normal, innocent, and peaceful that María Teresa almost succumbed to her worst defect: she very nearly let her attention stray. Then all of a sudden, just when it seemed that everyone's ties were properly tied, and the girls' ribbons correctly laced, she sees something that should never have happened and she should never have seen: Dreiman openly leaning on Baragli. She was leaning against his chest as she might have done against a wall, a bus-stop pole, or a lamp-post. It was not a wall or a post she was leaning on though, but Baragli, and what might have led to a quiet reprimand for untidiness, or for boys being boys, now seems to María Teresa like an out-of-tune note played in the middle of a harmonious concert. Despite being so shocked, or perhaps because she is so shocked, María Teresa reacts at once, and hurries over to where the scandal she wants to put an end to is going on. This is not something that demands a subtle approach, but decisiveness. It is not a case of Capelán perhaps brushing against Marré, the tension between watchfulness and stealth she is faced with every afternoon at the end of break. It is not that, it is Dreiman *clearly* leaning against Baragli, openly pressing her whole upper body against him, without the slightest compunction. There is nothing for María Teresa to consider or establish: she simply has to intervene, and in the most decisive manner possible.

—Dreiman: stand up straight.

Dreiman reacts in a suitably intimidated way. She

lowers her gaze at once, and in a sort of automatic reflex doubtless born of her sense of shame, smooths down her grey pleated skirt with both hands. She was not expecting to see the assistant out here on the pavement, under the tree branches by the roadside, and her surprise means she reacts instantaneously. María Teresa even imagines she sees Dreiman blush and swallow hard. She is not so sure that her intervention has been as successful as she would have liked, however, because unlike Dreiman, Baragli seems to find the whole affair highly amusing or even encouraging, and certainly not as a reason to feel ashamed of himself. He looks the assistant steadily in the eye, and seems about to smile, although he does not actually do so.

María Teresa decides to ignore Baragli and concentrate on Dreiman. After all, she was the one she reprimanded, and she was the one she had undoubtedly succeeded in impressing.

—Don't ever let me catch you doing that again, d'you hear?

Dreiman concurs. She somehow manages to keep her head down and yet to nod in agreement. Beside her, however, Baragli is still staring, almost defiantly, at María Teresa and is stifling a smile, or pretending to do so. María Teresa prefers to regard the incident as closed, and so walks away without giving the pupils any chance to think she is hesitating or being weak. However, something about the incident leaves her preoccupied or sad, so that a short while later, in the assistants' room, she chooses her words very carefully and raises the matter with Señor Biasutto.

Although he does not let go of the headed forms he has been studying, Señor Biasutto listens to her carefully and is obviously concerned.

—Do you know what? I'd really like us to discuss this matter later in a more relaxed manner.

María Teresa is gratified by his answer, although she is unsure whether Señor Biasutto is implying they should talk about the matter some other day, that week or the next, or whether he means a little later the same afternoon. In any case, it is impossible for her to discover what exactly Señor Biasutto was proposing, or for how long he wishes to postpone their conversation, because shortly after their exchange of words the school's normal daily routine is completely disrupted. It appeared to be a day like any other and, to a certain extent, it was. If there is anything the school guarantees above all else, it is this normality. Sometimes, however, things take such an unusual turn that, just as when rivers overflow their banks, they start to flood and invade even the most sheltered nooks and crannies. Nothing untoward ever happens at the school, and yet today, shortly after the second break, an urgent meeting is called of all the assistants from every year and class. And it is not Señor Biasutto who calls it, nor even the Head of Discipline – who María Teresa happens to catch a glimpse of hurrying towards the ground floor in an obviously agitated state. No, it is the highest authority in the school: the Deputy Headmaster, who has been acting head since the tragic death of the Headmaster.

More than thirty assistants are gathered in the main quad. To avoid showing how nervous they are, none of them glances up at the big clock with Roman numerals that presides over the courtyard, alongside the starched Argentinian flag and the austere bust of Manuel Belgrano, the creator of that flag and another former pupil. Nor do they exchange glances. They have formed a tight semi-circle, without necessarily being aware it was Señor Biasutto who encouraged them to do so. By the same token, this is the most appropriate way for them to hear what the Deputy Headmaster has to say without him having to raise his voice. The Head of Discipline is waiting to one side, and María Teresa forces herself not to look at his eyebrows, in fact not to look at him at all. At last the Deputy Headmaster arrives. Outwardly at least he appears calm. There is no need for him to raise his voice, something which in any case he never does. He reminds María Teresa of the parish priests she knew as a child in Villa del Parque: he knows how to convey the same sense of profound, protective calm. He is by no means skinny, however, and in that sense looks more like a bishop or a cardinal; nor has he ever been known to smile. But he has the same way of standing, as he is doing now, with both hands crossed in front of his body, and the same slow, deliberate way of speaking, as if delivering a sermon. All this gives him a venerable air that María Teresa noted the very first time she saw him. The sense of authority displayed by the Head of Discipline is quite different: he is the one who ensures that not so much as a piece of chalk is dropped in the school without him immediately becoming aware of it. Señor Biasutto's air of authority is different too: to everyone on the staff he is a kind of hero, because he is rumoured to have drawn up the lists, something of which everyone is aware.

The Deputy Headmaster by contrast is a father figure, although like the priests he is a symbolic rather than a real father: the virtual paternal figure of someone who has no children and has never known a woman. When the Deputy

23

Headmaster begins to speak it is with the same sense of measured wisdom. He makes hardly any gestures:

—Ladies and gentlemen: as Deputy Headmaster of the National School of Buenos Aires, I regret I have found it necessary to remove you from your usual daily duties. I had no alternative. At this moment, outside here – in the street, I mean – there are reports of disorder. Nothing that should worry us or oblige us to interrupt the normal course of our lessons. However, until the authorities succeed in re-establishing calm, which will doubtless occur in a very short time, we need to take preventative measures here within the school. I have to inform you that we have closed the main doors. By that I mean the ones which give on to Calle Bolívar. In consequence, after they have completed the timetables and activities scheduled for this afternoon in a normal fashion, the pupils are to leave school through the exit on Calle Moreno, which the Head of Discipline will indicate to you in due course. You should tell the pupils in your charge that they are at all costs to avoid the area of Plaza de Mayo. They will object that this is where they catch the metro. That does not matter: they must all, without exception, avoid going anywhere near Plaza de Mayo. As I have said, they are to leave by the Calle Moreno exit, and should head at once towards Avenida 9 de Julio. Be sure to tell them not to run, but not to loiter either. They are to leave as quickly as possible, but without running. Once they have reached Avenida 9 de Julio, they are to catch any bus that will get them out of this area, even if it does not take them directly home. Do not forget, ladies and gentlemen, that adolescents are by nature both curious and rebellious. Warn your pupils that they must on no account go near Plaza de Mayo, but be careful that in doing so you do not arouse their curiosity. What you must instil in them is fear, not curiosity. Tell them it is dangerous for them to go anywhere near Plaza de Mayo at the moment. If we evacuate the school calmly but quickly in the opposite direction, we will avoid any problems, and there will be no regrettable incidents.

At this, the Deputy Headmaster pauses. There is complete silence beneath school walls that are as dense as its history.

—Does anyone have any queries?

Nobody has any queries. Just in case, the Deputy Headmaster cups the smooth outline of his pallid chin in his hand, waiting for possible questions. What he expects is not that there will be any, but that there will be none. And nobody asks a question.

—No queries then. Perfect. Follow your instructions and have a good afternoon.

Third year class ten has Latin as the last period of the day. They are trying to scan some lines of verse: in a reluctant, uncoordinated chorus they stumble over rhythms in that essential but long-dead tongue. Their Latin master Mr Schulz beats the stresses with two fingers on the edge of his wooden desk, but this help either does not get through or is insufficient. Straight lines mean long syllables, cupped ones are short, but even though the rules for reading Latin verse out loud seem simple enough, there is no way that the tuneless chanting of the third year class ten pupils is going to sound harmonious. Listening to them out in the corridor, María Teresa is once again reminded of going to morning mass at the

Villa del Parque church as a young girl. The distressing sound has something of the Gregorian chant about it, but completely misses the meaning of the verses: none of them, and perhaps not even Mr Schulz, realises that somewhere in the thick of all this is Dido, and that Aeneas is searching for Dido, and that Aeneas is being written by Virgil, Mecenas is directing Virgil, and Mecenas himself is being controlled by Augustus, Emperor of Rome.

The bell goes for the end of lessons. Before they can leave, however, it is time for the lowering of the national flag. Strictly speaking, those doing this are the sixth-year pupils, already lined up in the central quad. Although the others – those in first, second, third, fourth and fifth years – stay in their classrooms and so are not directly involved in the ceremony, they know it is taking place, and this knowledge means that to some extent they are also taking part in the solemn act. The loudspeakers which play classical music during break times are now broadcasting the national anthem 'Aurora'. Standing to attention beside their desks, looking straight ahead at the assistants gazing back at them, every pupil in the school sings:

—This is the flag! Of my homeland! Born of the sun! That God has given me! It is the flag! Of my homeland! Born of the sun! That God has given me!

Today they are not leaving by the exit on to Calle Bolívar. Señor Biasutto coordinates his team of assistants, who in turn have already given instructions to the pupils so that this unusual procedure can be executed properly. In third year class ten, María Teresa manages to conceal her nervousness. Standing in the classroom doorway, she awaits orders. The classes file out one by one. Forms seven, eight, nine: finally it is her turn.

—All of you, follow me, Señor Biasutto instructs them.

To begin with, they take the usual route inside the school. Until they reach the big marble staircase leading down to the ground floor, nothing is any different to normal. But once they have left this behind – a procedure which demands they keep strictly in line – instead of carrying straight on and heading for the main entrance, they turn once again and reach the stairs leading down to the basement. These stairs are narrower and less well-lit, and until now María Teresa has never had to take them. The basement houses the gym, music room, the school canteen, as well as the swimming pool and a small cinema. Rumour has it that somewhere down here, perhaps beyond the gym, or in a passageway leading off from the cinema, there are secret tunnels that date back to the colonial era, when the National School was still the Royal School of San Carlos. The tunnels apparently led first to San Ignacio Church, and then on to the Plaza Mayor fortress, or as it is today, to the presidential palace at the far end of Plaza de Mayo.

When her group reaches the basement, María Teresa feels a certain apprehension. Even though this low-ceilinged world is only slightly gloomier than the rest of the cloisters and annexes, when she tries to make out where the tunnels might begin she has the sense of something sinister. Señor Biasutto's voice snaps her out of her troubled thoughts.

—Quickly, down this way.

The door out on to Calle Moreno is small and scarcely noticeable in the greyish wall of which it is part. Perhaps it is secret as well, like the hidden tunnels that give rise to so much speculation. In fact, it is never opened or used, except on rare occasions like today.

—Until tomorrow, ladies and gentlemen.

The pupils launch themselves into the street like parachutists falling from an aeroplane: scared but aware there is no going back. They will do as they are told: leave the area without stopping, but without rushing either. They will go home. Once their tasks for the day have been completed, the assistants will also go home. At half-past six in the evening, they fetch their belongings and hasten to leave the school. It is only then, when she realises they will all have to return to the basement, that María Teresa understands that the instructions the Deputy Head gave, and which they faithfully passed on to the pupils, also affect and include them. She also has to leave by the side door on to Calle Moreno. She also cannot take the metro where she normally gets it. She also will hurry (but without running) towards Avenida 9 de Julio. There she also will take the first bus that comes, even if she will then have to get off and change to another that goes to her home. She does not know either what exactly is going on, although she behaves with the determination of someone who does. She has no real inkling.

The street looks calm. Too calm, in fact: that is what is odd about it. This is the rush hour, and yet here, right in the heart of Buenos Aires, only one or two vehicles pass her by. The pedestrians seem to María Teresa to have just emerged from cellars, as if they were scurrying from one shelter to another along the streets of a city under attack from the air. They are taking advantage of an all-clear, but still have a stunned look on their faces. Of course, María Teresa might have the same expression on her face, but she cannot see herself. If she had to distinguish a sign that hinted at what was happening, she would be unable to do so. Yet there can be no doubt that the sky above the city has darkened, that as night approaches a heavy pall has fallen. Impossible to tell precisely where this sense of foreboding comes from, but it is as palpable as the air itself.

María Teresa finally reaches Avenida 9 de Julio. She wonders if it can be true that it is the widest avenue in the world. She looks left and right, trying to spot a bus she can catch. When she looks right, she sees the Obelisk, and this reminds her of the postcard her brother sent. Remembering that image leaves her thinking of him.

3

Servelli repeats his well-known habit, that of bursting out laughing for no reason at all; but this time he does so at the worst possible moment. This inane laughter, which so delights his companions, and has to be reprimanded, is due either to nerves, to a wish to seem guileless, or to the fact that he is always slow to understand jokes or sarcastic comments. It is a laugh which usually provokes more mocking guffaws from his classmates. This time, however, the circumstances are so obviously awkward that the laugh explodes and subsides all on its own, foundering in a general atmosphere of scandalized silence.

The Head of Discipline is going round all the afternoon classes to say a few words to every pupil. When he comes into the room, they should all stand up and stand quietly to attention by the side of their desks. They also do this when a teacher comes in, but then they sit down again for the start of the lesson, whereas now they have to stay on their feet, eyes to the front and arms by their sides, until such time as the Head of Discipline has finished speaking and taken his leave of the classroom.

His words are few, but carefully chosen and delivered with an emphasis that lends them conviction. They refer to what the National School of Buenos Aires means to the history of the Republic of Argentina, and consequently what it means to be a pupil there. They refer to the past: the school's foundation in the year 1778 by Viceroy Vértiz (the second viceroy of what were then the United Provinces of the Río de la Plata), the man who became known to posterity as the Viceroy of the Enlightenment (partly because he inaugurated the first street lighting in Buenos Aires, and partly because he established the pillars of Enlightenment belief, such as the Royal School of San Carlos). The Head of Discipline goes on to outline a brief roll-call of famous former pupils from the era when the school was known as the School of Moral Sciences, among whom undoubtedly the most illustrious was one of the nation's founding fathers, Manuel Belgrano, member of the 1810 independence junta, victor at the battles of Salta and Tucumán, and, inspired by its clear blue skies, the creator of the flag of Argentina. The school, he reminds them, was successfully refounded in 1863, now to be known as the National School, thanks to the foresight of Bartolomé Mitre, another founding father of the nation; the first president of modern-day Argentina, an outstanding soldier, a considerable historian, a born journalist and a practised translator. Mitre founded the nation, but also the newspaper *La Nación*, the written history of the nation, and the National School. Later still, towards 1880, the school was the cradle for the most brilliant generation in the history of Argentina, as revealed by Miguel Cané is his now classic *Juvenilia*: yet again, the school played a decisive role in the unfolding consolidation of the Argentinian state.

The Head of Discipline declares that in this short overview he has clearly demonstrated that the history of the fatherland and the history of the school are one and the same. This demonstration leads to the inevitable conclusion that each and every pupil at the school (from the mere fact of being one) is uniquely committed to being a patriot, more so than any other Argentinian (those Argentinians, he stresses, who are worthy of the birthright). When the fatherland calls, the most rapid, most reliable response will come from the pupils of this school.

—I want you to reflect on this. Especially at this moment.

With this, the Head of Discipline concludes his remarks. He takes his leave, and is about to step out of the classroom. He has crossed the threshold, but is not yet completely outside, so that he is still part of whatever happens in the class. And what happens is unthinkable, something that should never have occurred: for no reason whatsoever, inanely, Servelli bursts out laughing. A short, hollow laugh. There is no malice to it, and yet it is clear and perfectly audible. The Head of Disicpline halts in the doorway. For a brief moment, he stands stock still. His back is to the class, but doubtless his eyebrow is twitching furiously. For one second, he does not move. This is not a moment's hesitation, but one of disbelief. Immediately afterwards, the Head of Discipline turns, retraces his steps, comes back into the room. He steps up onto the platform at the front once more, from where he has a clear view of the entire class. He folds his hands behind his back. His middle finger is shaking. Not even the sound of creaking floorboards can be heard. The Head of Discipline demands:

—Who was it?

No-one replies. His mouth sets in a grim line. He nods repeatedly, as though he is beginning to understand something that leaves him unmoved.

—I want the person responsible to speak up.

The tic in his eyebrow leads him to give an involuntary blink, undermining his stern expression. No-one admits responsibility.

—Whoever knows who it was, speak now.

The Head of Discipline's neck twists; his teeth seem to be searching for something in his mouth. Nobody says a word. They all know it was Servelli, because he is the one who laughs when nobody else does. But none of them says a thing. María Teresa is very close to the Head of Discipline, also facing the class, although she is not on the platform. She is confused: she also knows that the pupil who laughed was Servelli. She wonders what she should do: speak up or not? There is no time for hesitation: if she is going to say something, she has to do so straightaway. She does not know what to do. On the one hand she is afraid (quite rightly) that if she stays quiet the pupils will take her silence for complicity, because they know that she knows. So she should declare at once: 'It was Servelli.' On the other, she senses that what the Head of Discipline wants is not simply to discover who laughed, but something far beyond that: he wants the culprit to confess, or one of his classmates to tell on him. For this to happen, María Teresa would do best to keep out of it. When the Head of Discipline asks who it was, when the Head of Discipline wants to know if any of them knows who it was, he is not including her among those he is addressing. She is the assistant for third year class ten, not one of the pupils. In order to maintain this vital distinction, she has to stay completely silent. And so this is what she does, partly because she has decided to say nothing, and partly because she is still hesitating when the Head of Discipline decides he has waited long enough, and takes action:

—Third year class ten will receive a collective punishment. You are all to stay behind for the seventh hour for the whole week.

There are six periods of classes each day, and each period lasts forty minutes. With the three breaks, this makes up the five hours that the afternoon session lasts: from ten minutes past one when school starts, to ten minutes past six, when it finishes. However, for either pedagogical or disciplinary reasons, the school authorities can add an extra hour, the seventh hour. In these cases, the pupils have to remain at school until close to seven in the evening. By this time, the building is empty, or almost, and the unmistakable air of desolation only adds to the sense of punishment. The echo of distant footsteps can be heard, and there is clear evidence that in the streets outside night is falling or has already fallen. During this seventh hour, the pupils have to remain in their classrooms, seated at their desks. They are not permitted to talk, or to do anything that is not school work. They may study if they wish, but if they do not want to do so, they cannot do anything else.

—This is not a free period, ladies and gentlemen.

Nor may they pass each other notes, chew gum, undo their uniforms in any way, or play any kind of game, even on their own.

—This is not a reward. It is not break-time, it is a punishment.

The seventh hour is also difficult for the assistants, precisely because nothing at all happens, and it is this nothing they have to oversee. María Teresa is now sitting in the teachers' chair, up on the platform, looking directly at the class. The pupils are still and silent: most of them are

34

doing nothing. They do not yet have any written work to hand in, so that although the pupils should always be able to find something to complete or at least make progress with, they have no pressing deadlines. A few of them are reading, or chewing the end of a pen as they puzzle over an equation they are unlikely to solve. Several others are simply staring into space, letting the time go by. Depending on the point of view, the punishment of this seventh hour consists either of having to spend more time studying in school, or as having to put up with the passage of time: watching time go by, and nothing else.

María Teresa is making sure that none of the pupils are finding ways to enjoy the seventh hour.

—What are you doing, Valentinis?

—Reading, Miss.

—I can see that, Valentinis. I want to know what you're reading. Is it a magazine?

—I'm reading about music, Miss.

—Is it something Mr Roel gave you?

—No, Miss.

—Do you mean to say that what you are reading has nothing to do with your music lesson?

—No, Miss.

—Put it away then.

One problem of the seventh hour is that whereas the pupils can choose to either get on with something or simply sit staring at nothing until seven o'clock comes round, even if they would like to, the assistants are unable to do anything apart from sit and watch. María Teresa takes her time studying the pupils' faces (if there is one thing she has, it is time). She considers Capelán, for instance: the

35

fluttering of his hands or fingers on Marré's shoulder is repeated whenever they line up and step apart; she would love to be able to discover in his features (as the great nineteenth-century scientists aspired to do) a principle of either innocence or guilt that would settle the matter so that she did not have to continue keeping an eye on him. After this, she concentrates on Servelli. He is the one to blame for the fact that all his classmates have been punished and are still here, in detention and bored beyond belief, and yet she can detect nothing in his expression or behaviour that betrays any sign of remorse. Next she studies Cascardo: the book he is reading apparently requires so much effort that his ears are suddenly glowing red. They look as if they are about to catch fire. She gazes at other faces, most of which are blank, then starts the process over again. As long as there are no interruptions or changes to this exercise of her powers of observation, María Teresa intends to continue with it until it is close enough to seven o'clock for her to stop. She does not expect any shocks. And yet the assistant, who is the one meant to observe, suddenly senses that she herself is being observed. At first she cannot discover who it is, but she is certain it is happening, because that is how these things are; she raises her eyes, determined to find out which eyes are fixed on her. And the person staring at her from his desk is none other than Baragli. Yes, Baragli is staring straight at her, although his look could also be one of complete boredom. That is how María Teresa would like to see it, although there is something (she cannot be sure what) that niggles her. She would like to see it as nothing more than a blank look, a harmless lapse, the lazy indolence of having nothing whatsoever to do. She would like to interpret it in this way, yet there is something that stops her. She is not sure what exactly. She cannot decide whether it is sarcasm, or worse still, lust, because if it were either of these she could intervene decisively and put an immediate stop to it (no matter that it is impossible to interpret the meaning of a look precisely: her word would be enough, and there could be no room for appeal). No, Baragli is not mocking her; nor is he, strictly speaking, giving her a male look; and yet María Teresa is convinced his gaze is not entirely innocent. He is not trying to provoke her: if she were to react, that would be going too far. It is plain though that Baraglia is staring at her too much, for too long, and in too fixed a way. He is doing so in such a subtle manner, however, that if accused he could claim he was simply staring into space, not looking at anything in particular, at the blackboard, the wall, or the ceiling, that strictly speaking he was staring straight ahead, which was no offence, and that it was not his fault that she happened to be directly in front of him. María Teresa is aware of these possibilities, and so decides to do nothing. She tries to look at something else, at other faces, or to stare vaguely at the back wall in the same way as they, the pupils, are expected to gaze at the front one, but eyes that are staring at you possess an irresistible attraction (as History of Art students well know), and so sooner or later she finds herself glancing in Baragli's direction once more. Baragli is still staring at her. María Teresa lowers her gaze a fraction: not to move away from Baragli, but to observe his mouth. She discovers what she suspected: the start of a highly disturbing smile. If it were a proper laugh, or even a full smile, if there were a clear signal at the corners of his mouth, it would be easy for her to step in, take action, punish Baragli and declare the matter closed. But she cannot take steps against a gesture that does not yet exist. Which is about to exist, which she can intuit and even predict, but which does not yet exist. There is nothing she can do except wait. Wait until it is almost seven o'clock. Finally that moment arrives, and the seventh hour is over.

—Very good. Collect your things.

The pupils start leaving the room. María Teresa stands in the doorway to supervise them. Her position allows her simultaneously to monitor the cloister and the classroom, the pupils who have already left as well as those who have not yet done so. Of course, it also means they all have to pass quite close to her. One or two even brush against her (without meaning to) with their satchel or a blazer sleeve. When Baragli goes by, he does not look at her. Strangely or not (she cannot make up her mind), he does not even glance at her. He goes by quickly, apparently oblivious to everything apart from the floor and his shoes. As he passes by, however, the smell he gives off brings memories flooding into her mind. All of a sudden, María Teresa finds herself transported back to evenings in her childhood home. It takes her a few seconds to realise it is her father she is remembering: her father after supper, when she was a little girl, when they lived in a house with a back garden and flowerbeds. Startled by the association, it takes a little longer for her to link Baragli passing by with an identical smell from those long-lost nights, and to identify it as the smell of black tobacco. Her father used to smoke that kind of cigarette, which came in gold- and green-striped packets; nowadays they are not so common, but you can still buy them. Every night, the smell of the spirals of smoke filled her childhood home because they were part of an unalterable ritual. And now, as he went by her, Baragli brought this smell back to her, or rather brought her back to the smell, with the result that she stands lost in thought, or lost for thought, in the doorway, at the edge of the end of the day.

When she leaves the school shortly afterwards, and later still as she is travelling on the metro, she cannot free herself from what has just taken place in her memory, which is acting exactly as a smell usually does: something which sticks to your clothes or in your nostrils, and which lasts beyond any rational calculation. She is dismayed at first to find she is so susceptible, to discover that a mere incident at school can affect her so much, even hurt her. Then she is also upset to realise how long her unease is lasting: she passes one station after another, leaving the school and what occurred there increasingly far behind, yet in spite of this she cannot escape from the world that sprang up out of that simple fleeting smell: the world of that house, the garden, the flowerbeds, night, childhood, her father, tobacco, the smell of smoke, Baragli.

She manages to recover her composure only when she is able to see the incident from the point of view of her function: that of assistant to third year class ten. She should have seen it this way from the start, but it is only now she becomes aware of it. From the standpoint of the assistant in charge of discipline for her form, there is another reason for this incident to worry her. It is both simple and obvious, but until the moment she thinks of it in this way, it had completely escaped her: if the pupil Baragli, at seven in the evening no less, passed by her reeking of tobacco, that must mean he was smoking, and smoking not only inside the school, but during class hours.

María Teresa is pleased with her deductions. She does not reproach herself for not having done so earlier, at the very moment she should have done. Rather than blaming herself for anything, she congratulates herself. Everything else is simply a question of time: this is what she decides. That is because at this precise moment, this evening, in this gloomy tunnel beneath the city, she takes the crucial decision about what will be her most important task over the coming days: to catch Baragli, and those who are behaving like him, in the act of breaking the rules: in other words, as is commonly said, and as she herself thinks of it, to catch them *in flagrante*.

And so when Señor Biasutto comes up to her one quiet afternoon in the assistants' room and somewhat to her surprise reminds her that they still have a matter to discuss, María Teresa prefers not to mention the original episode she intended to bring up – the suggestive way in which Dreiman was leaning against Baragli on the pavement outside the school when she saw them, or to inform him of her most persistent concern, which is that there are pupils who take advantage of the stepping-apart manoeuvre to slyly touch each other in prohibited ways. Instead, she refers to this more recent and much more serious infraction, namely that she strongly suspects, in fact is almost sure, that there are pupils who are finding a way to smoke during school hours, on the school premises. Señor Biasutto, who was listening to her standing up, comes and sits next to her.

—I'm extremely interested in what you're saying.

María Teresa is relieved to hear this, then finds that

her relief quickly changes to enthusiasm; and shortly afterwards, that her enthusiasm has turned into a sense of pride. Señor Biasutto, the supervisor in charge of all the assistants, is pleased with her work. He agrees with her, listens to her, thinks her suspicions are well-founded and worth taking into account.

It may be that in other schools this kind of transgression is admissible, or is even seen as commonplace: that pupils hide in the toilets to smoke is a cliché. But the National School aims to be an exception, even in a matter such as this. Señor Biasutto speaks with the authority of all the time he has been in his post, and his quiet pride in the work he has been able to achieve. He has years of experience, and it is out of this experience (as if he were up on the raised platform the teachers occupy to give their lessons) that he now talks to María Teresa. She is the newest assistant, and yet despite this she has shown (and he should know) the most remarkable aptitude for her work.

Señor Biasutto tells her these have been the most difficult years for both school and country. A period that fortunately appears to have been left behind, although to count on this would be the worst mistake imaginable. María Teresa thinks this might be the moment to ask him about the lists, to ask him how he drew them up; in the end, however, she does not have the courage, and says nothing. Señor Biasutto has come up with a comparison: subversion, he explains to her as a newcomer, is like a cancer. A cancer which first affects one organ, for example, the youth of a country, infecting it with violence and foreign ideas; but soon the cancer spreads, goes into what is known as metastasis, and although the effects may be less serious, they still have to be fought against, because the roots of cancer are still there, and cancer is not defeated until all traces of it have been cut out. Señor Biasutto slowly strokes his dark moustache, as if remembering. The time has gone, he says, when we had to uncover illegal activities and seize highly dangerous material (One of these days, he whispers in María Teresa's ear, I'll show you some of it: I've kept it all in a file on 'ideological infiltration'). Like the country, our school has been able triumphantly to leave those days behind, but what use would it be to have got rid of the cancer if we do not continue to keep a close lookout for any chance that it might have left traces?

Señor Biasutto makes a movement, but does not complete it, which leaves María Teresa perplexed. She might have understood it if he had gone through with it: she thinks it was intended as a move to lay the firm, wise hand of the irreproachable, experienced supervisor on her newcomer's arm. But his hand comes to a halt in mid-air, as if overtaken by amnesia. At the same time, he launches into another comparison: subversion is a body, but it is also a spirit. Because a spirit survives and can be reincarnated in another body. What does smoking in the school toilets mean? Señor Biasutto pauses, but María Teresa has understood that this is a rhetorical question. At another time, or even in another school, he says in answer to himself, it is no more than a bit of mischief: the typical mischief of wayward adolescence. But at this moment, and in this school, it is something else: it is the spirit of subversion returning to threaten us.

Señor Biasutto smooths down his hair with both hands, pleased because he feels he has expressed exactly what he meant to say. He knows María Teresa is starting to admire him, perhaps even before she realises it herself.

42

4

Her mother cries more frequently than ever now, sobbing and choking. Throughout the day, but especially in the morning, the radio browbeats its listeners with military marches. Another postcard has arrived from Francisco. The same picture as before: a panorama of the Obelisk in Buenos Aires. It could have been another similar photograph, but in fact it is exactly the same one. María Teresa proves it by comparing the red bus going round the base of the Obelisk. The same photo and the same joke: pretending he is far away, or that they, his mother and sister, are far off, so that this card from Buenos Aires would suggest travel. On the back, Francisco has also repeated the same phrase as before: 'I can't seem to make friends.'

Francisco must have written these words on the table of some makeshift barracks, probably, but incorrectly, called a 'canteen', and used another postcard from a pack bought by the dozen. Since what was important for him was to make a joke, rather than that they should find it funny, he sees no problem in repeating that too. It is obvious he is amusing himself rather than trying to give his mother or sister any pleasure. What he does not imagine, or take into account, is that the postal service is also involved, and that as a result his note is considerably delayed. By the time

43

María Teresa takes the letter from the kitchen table, when it is opened and read with unnecessary anxiety, the joke he was making has become true: he is a long way off. He is not on the outskirts of Buenos Aires in Villa Martelli now. He has been transferred. Without warning or explanation (and no reason why they should give them) he and the others were ordered to collect their things, fill their packs, and to form up on the parade ground. From there they were told to climb up onto the backs of several snub-nosed trucks, sheltered only by some poorly-tied tarpaulins. They were not going far, although it was not close by either: to a place called Azul. It took hours for them to get there.

María Teresa tries to comfort her mother, who mostly listens but does not hear her, or else hears but does not understand, or even understands but does not believe her, with a simple but obviously inadequate explanation: that although it is true that Azul is south of Buenos Aires, it is not in the south of Argentina. María Teresa has looked at a map: she found one at school, because although year three does not do the geography of Argentina, year five does. Azul is in Buenos Aires province, more or less in the middle, further north than the sudden hills of the Sierra de la Ventana, and above all far, very far, from the sea. The mother bursts into tears anyway and wonders what on earth will happen next.

At school the top priority is to maintain discipline and keep the pupils focused on their work. This does not mean that the possible outcomes of the events going on outside are ignored. In fact, the Deputy Headmaster has ordered that everyone, pupils and staff, must wear the blue-and-white Argentinian rosette in their lapels. However, in a place of study, that is what must be the top priority. The afternoon when, for some unknown reason, the siren on the *La Prensa* newspaper building went off (which, because of its proximity to the school, sounded as if were coming over the cloister loudspeakers), there were groans and a vague fear that the city was being bombarded. The expression on the faces of even the teachers, or perhaps above all of the teachers, changed to one of studied concern or outright fear, when they heard a sound they had previously only encountered in films. That afternoon, the *La Prensa* siren blared out for almost a minute, without anyone ever discovering why: whether it had gone off accidentally or was being tested. Usually, the only sound capable of penetrating the school's thick, historic walls and the hermetic sealing of the constantly closed windows is the ringing of the bell signalling exactly each hour, half hour, a quarter past and a quarter to the hour, from the former city hall tower, which plays the exact same tune as Big Ben in London. Apart from this meticulous measurement of the passage of time from only a block away from the school, the days in the building flow by as though it were not situated in the heart of the city of Buenos Aires, but in the middle of a desert.

Nothing making a noise outside succeeds in resonating within the school. But the siren of *La Prensa* in the famous tower that adds so much lustre to Avenida de Mayo sounded as if it were coming from right inside. Worse still, inside the school everyone fell silent, waiting for what was going to happen next. The sound lasted for almost a minute. Then there was silence once more, and nothing happened. Nothing. There was a smattering of nervous laughter, something almost unheard of in the school. Even some of the teachers laughed, or perhaps especially the teachers did so. Following that minute, lessons resumed as though nothing had occurred; no-one imagined there could be any other possibility, and in fact there was none. It was only during Rosa's dictatorship, the worst tragedy in the entire nineteenth-century history of Argentina, that teaching in the school had been interrupted, and nothing similar could ever be allowed to happen, not even for a single day.

María Teresa starts carrying out her plan to keep a watch on the toilets during the school breaks. Normally the assistants roam the cloisters at random, while the students spend the time chatting, going over their work, or taking the opportunity to buy something to eat from the tuck shops situated on every floor of the school. As she strolls around observing the pupils, María Teresa still gives the appearance of not going anywhere in particular: a few steps down this way, then back that way, as is typical of any patrol. In fact, though, her route is no longer entirely random: she is concentrating above all on that part of the cloister on the second floor which houses the toilets. There are two of them on each floor, one for girls and one for boys. Each toilet has two doors, one at each end. The doors have two green-painted wooden leaves that swing open and closed, like the ones in the Westerns she sees on Saturday evening television. Swing doors that do not reach the ground but only about as far as the pupils' thighs. They have to be pushed open with the shoulder or by using a hand, and then swing back and forth as their name suggests, slowly subsiding until they come to rest exactly opposite each other.

María Teresa focuses on the boys' toilet. If, as she

suspects, there are pupils smoking at school, this must be where they do it. The assistants always walk along slowly, calmly, but in a determined fashion. She usually speeds up a little when she goes past the toilet doors: she will have to make sure she no longer does that. Without coming to a halt (which would be improper) she has to pause outside the doors in order to be able to detect what she wants to detect. She looks down at the ground: the last thing she needs is for it to seem as though she is peering inside the boys' toilet – something which, given the way the swing doors flap, would be quite possible. No, she does not want to look inside, but to sniff out whether the school regulations are being flouted in the secrecy of the toilets. This would of course be easier for a male assistant, because he could go inside, but María Teresa has no wish to share her suspicions with any male colleague, with Marcelo or Leonardo, or Alberto. She wants to be the one who discovers the culprit, and can present the case as solved for Señor Biasutto's doubtless admiring consideration.

A strong smell of bleach always wafts out of the toilets. Even though it is almost chokingly strong, it is a clean smell. As the school day progresses, this smell naturally fades, due to the continual use of the toilets and the passage of time, and yet it is never completely covered by the kind of toilet smells always present in trains or certain bars. At most, by the end of the day there is a kind of neutral situation, suggesting neither hygiene nor the lack of it: in other words, there is the smell of nothing, or the complete lack of any smell.

However that may be, there is never anything – either at the start, the middle, or the end of the school day – that

47

suggests the smell of black tobacco. There is no lingering trace that a pupil may have lit a cigarette in the relative privacy of the cubicles, breathing in the smoke and then puffing it out, or blowing it out without even drawing it into his lungs, as happens with many adolescents who smoke, or think they do. After her father, Francisco was the only person María Teresa has seen smoking close by her.

Señor Biasutto did not show much interest in her proposal, and does not know she is busy pursuing it. However, María Teresa is well aware that if she can find positive evidence of the irregularities which so far are mere supposition, the chief assistant will not merely be pleased, but grateful towards her. He seems particularly busy these days: perhaps that is why he has not said anything to her. Even so, when they meet in the corridor or in the assistants' room, he always makes a point of gesturing towards her. This is usually a rather vague wave of the hand, but it appears to show appreciation or deference, or at the very least that he has not forgotten the special conversation they had a few days earlier.

It is a time when great emphasis is being put on school work. There is a lot to do throughout the school day, because there is a sense that without this strenuous effort, things could go awry. And there is nothing more valued at the school than routine. Free periods, for example, generally tolerated as an accidental emergency, are now completely ruled out. Usually, the schoolteachers are never absent. Stories are told of all those who came to give their classes despite being ill or convalescent, or only hours after having suffered the irreparable loss of a loved one, because they preferred to miss a check-up or a funeral rather than miss school. In spite of this, and because every rule must have its exception, very occasionally a teacher does not turn up. Of course, he or she has to inform the school in good time, and this is always done with genuine remorse, but their absence inevitably means there are free periods in the timetable. Behaviour in these free classes is governed by the same rules as during the seventh hours, although the assistants always claim that these free classes are not free time. The Deputy Headmaster, who is in charge of timetabling, has brought in a change regarding any such free periods (a change designed to ensure normality is maintained, to be sure that nothing disturbs the sovereign call of study). Whenever a teacher is going to be absent, it is his or her responsibility to inform the assistants of the affected classes not only of their absence but also to supply them with work that the pupils can get on with during the periods which, despite everything, are still called free. The assistants are responsible for handing out this work, making sure the pupils do it, and then taking it in and later sending it to the absent teacher.

María Teresa has to sit at the teacher's desk up on the platform for third year class ten, because Mr Cano, their history teacher, is not going to be in today. She has to cover two periods: the fifth and six, the last in the school day. For the first time, María Teresa uses the double blackboard she has so often stared at, which, thanks to a system that for some reason reminds her of the theatre world, allows one board to rise while the other drops, and vice versa. She rubs hesitantly with the board-duster to erase a two-sided equation that apparently left all the pupils baffled in the previous lesson. Mr Cano, who in recent classes had been teaching about the Punic Wars, has left work to be done in case he is absent. It is an exercise in analyzing and discussing historical quotations.

At first, the chalk dust hovering in the air after María Teresa has rubbed the board clean makes it a little hard to read what she is writing. She begins: 'Read the following quotations carefully. Then comment on them and relate them to each other.' She coughs or clears her throat, then explains that there are twelve quotes, which she is going to dictate to them. She does so with the same methodical slowness as she patrols the cloisters during break-time. Even so, there is always someone who is slow at writing and asks her to wait. Or someone who does not catch the last words she says, and wants her to repeat them.

The first quote Mr Cano has left and which María Teresa is now dictating to the third year class ten pupils is from Sun Tzu. Before reading it out loud, she turns and writes on the blackboard, printing so that it is more legible: 'Sun Tzu. *The Art of War*.' Then she starts to dictate: 'The essence of martial arts is discretion.' She pauses, then repeats: 'The essence . . . of martial . . . arts . . . is discretion.' Next quotation: 'Deception is a weapon of war.' A pause, then: 'Deception . . . is a weapon . . . of war.' Third quotation, linked to the previous one: 'Bear in mind that your enemies also employ deception.' She pauses. Repeats: 'Bear in mind . . . your enemies . . . also employ . . . deception.' Fourth quotation.

'Is this still Sun Tzu?'

'Yes, Valenzuela. Until I tell to you the contrary, the quotations all come from *The Art of War* by Sun Tzu. Fourth quotation: 'Do not harass a desperate enemy.' She pauses, repeats: 'Do not . . . harass . . . a desperate . . . enemy.' Fifth quote: 'Total victory is not having to fight a battle.' Pause, repetition: 'Total victory . . . is not . . . having to fight . . . a battle.'

All the quotes so far are from Sun Tzu. Now María Teresa turns to the blackboard again and writes directly beneath what she wrote before: 'Niccolo Machiavelli: *On the Art of War*.' She dictates the sixth quote, the first from Machiavelli: 'What keeps an army united is the fame of its general.' She pauses. Then repeats slowly: 'What keeps . . . an army . . . united . . . is the fame . . . of its general.' Seventh quote, the second from Machiavelli: 'One must try not to push the enemy into a desperate position.' A pause. She says again: 'One must try . . . not to push . . . the enemy . . . into a . . . desperate position.' Now for the third author. María Teresa writes on the blackboard: Karl von Clausewitz: *On War*. Eighth quote, the first from Clausewitz.

—Wait, please.

Eighth quotation, the first from Clausewitz. 'War is the province of chance.' A pause, then she says again: 'War . . . is the . . . province . . . of chance.'

—Could you repeat that?

—No. You can copy it from your neighbour afterwards.

Ninth quote, also from Clausewitz. She dictates: 'War implies uncertainty.' She pauses, repeats: 'War . . . implies . . . uncertainty.' Tenth quotation. Third and last from Clausewitz. 'In many wars action takes up the lesser amount of time, and inaction the greater part.' She pauses. Repeats: 'In many wars . . . action takes up . . . the lesser amount . . . of time . . . and inaction . . . the greater part.' María Teresa could use the pulleys (which so remind her of backstage at

51

the theatre) to make sure that the part of the blackboard she now has to write on is at chest-level, but instead she bends down. And it is from this awkward position that she writes (her handwriting rather more shaky because she has to stretch) the quote from the last writer on the list: Mao Tse Tung: *Military Writings*. Then she dictates the eleventh quote: 'All those who participate in a war must free themselves from their usual habits and become used to war.' María Teresa pauses, then repeats: 'All those . . . who participate . . . in a war . . . must free themselves . . . from their usual habits . . . and become used . . . to war.' Finally she dictates the last quote for their work, which is by the same author: 'We admit that the phenomenon of war is the riskiest and offers less certainty than any other social phenomenon.' A pause. She repeats: 'We admit . . . that the . . . phenomenon . . . of war . . . is the riskiest . . . and offers . . . less certainty . . . than any other . . . social . . . phenomenon.'

María Teresa leaves the sheet of paper with the quotations prepared by Mr Cano on the desk. Everything the pupils need has been written on the blackboard.

—Any questions?

None.

—No questions?

None.

—Very good. Now get on with it.

The pupils lower their heads and start writing. Some sit there, pens between their teeth, waiting to find the words to express their ideas. María Teresa watches them all, but her mind wanders. It is the last lesson of the day.

The next postcard they receive from Francisco is sent

from Azul. It looks as if he bought this one himself. He must have got it new, but its edges are already worn, as if someone had used it as a bookmark in a bulky novel, although it is more likely that nobody ever used it for this or any other purpose, and that the slight crease and fold at its corners are simply due to the card having been kept for so long in the metal rack of a village shop, handled and finally rejected by a whole series of travelling salesmen, long-distance bus drivers, or supply teachers. The picture on the front must be of the main square in Azul. In its centre is the obligatory statue of General José de San Martín perched on his horse, arm raised from his shoulder, finger raised from his hand, pointing towards the far horizon. The edges of the photograph show rows of exuberant flowers, their colours retouched to make the photo more attractive. María Teresa is already prepared to find no more than a few words written by her brother. This time, however, there is nothing: he has not written a thing. Nothing apart from his first name, his signature: Francisco.

No-one at the school knows María Teresa has a brother. There is of course no reason why they should, since in addition to the usual discretion shown at work, she adds a personal shyness and reserve. In the assistants' room she follows other people's conversations, but herself says little, and what she does come out with are usually nothing more than polite stock phrases (How terrible! Who would have thought it! I can't believe it! God forbid!) At break-time, the assistants are on their own so that they can patrol a wider area, and therefore do not talk to each other. In addition, María Teresa is now making it her duty to visit the sector of the toilets that most of the others try to avoid.

53

She is determined to keep up her furtive supervision. She repeatedly lingers there, although she is careful not to show any particular concern. For the moment, she has not found any proof. The smell from the toilets is still that of bleach, in which predominates what she takes to be ammonia, or occasionally a dense but odourless atmosphere.

To make things worse, with the approach of winter the weather in Buenos Aires has been turning colder, and the sudden gusts of wind in the streets have given her a stubborn cold. She is forced always to take a handkerchief with her, discreetly concealed between the tight sleeve of her black pullover and the white cuffs of her blouse, which she uses to blow her nose time and again. She blows so hard she can feel her ears pop, but even so her nostrils almost immediately become congested again, and are never really clear. As a result, she cannot smell properly: she is sure that lots of subtleties escape her. Even so, she reassures herself that the scent of tobacco, if it existed, would not escape her, even at a distance.

The comings and goings in the toilets are very odd, although María Teresa only notices this now that she is keeping a close watch on them. Some pupils go to the toilet every break-time; a few even enter more than once in the same break. Some others never visit them: they seem not to need to. Some spend several minutes inside, obviously because they are in great need; others come and go so quickly that María Teresa is left wondering how these boys can possibly relieve themselves in so short a time, although like everyone else she is well aware that it is not so complicated for boys as for girls, and that there is no need, *a posteriori*, for the same amount of hygiene. As she walks past the swing doors she hears boys' voices inside, but she does not want to hear things, she wants to smell them. Even so, every time she goes by she does hear things (she does not want to see either, or to look, yet sometimes her eyes wander of their own accord through the double doors, where almost against her will she catches sight of flashes of legs, fleeting backs, hands in movement). María Teresa can make out the sound of voices, and conversations: apparently boys do not behave in the same way as girls when they go to the toilet. Girls talk before and after they relieve themselves, but during the act itself they prefer to be on their own, thinking their own thoughts, and renouncing the existence of everyone else. María Teresa imagines that boys on the other hand are involved in a strange mixture of intimacy and social life: she has the impression that they do not interrupt their conversations while they are doing whatever they have to do, and can even laugh at a joke another boy has made, or allow their companion to clap them on the back in a friendly way, or even look each other in the face as they would in a normal conversation. It is only now, since she has begun her patrols, that this crosses María Teresa's mind; until now her thoughts about this kind of thing were very different, or more exactly, she never thought about it.

5

The Head of Discipline has called an inspection. It is important to hold one (without prior warning, of course) every so often, because however much effort is put into creating and upholding values, behaviour tends to become lax. These inspections have two main focal points: hair and stockings. Every assistant is well aware of the regulations in both these cases. However, it is one thing to know what the regulation says, quite another to make sure they are being followed sufficiently strictly. The girls have to wear their hair up, in plaits or a pony tail. It must be kept in place with hair-slides and a blue hairband. Fringes are not permitted (although not openly stated, it is generally believed that a clear brow is a sign of intelligence). The boys must have short hair: this means it must be above the ears, and must be the width of two normal-sized fingers above the collar. All pupils' stockings must be blue and made of nylon. It is easy to check that the girls meet this requirement, because they wear jumpers and skirts, so that their stockings are clearly visible. In the boys' case, it is more difficult, particularly when their thick, grey trousers reach down to their black moccasin shoes. In order for the inspection to be carried out, they have to stretch one leg forward, then the other, each time lifting the leg of their trouser a little way. This manoeuvre requires a certain delicacy, which naturally the boys hate. María Teresa walks down the line of pupils formed up in the quad: they have already stepped apart and are standing to attention. All the girls' stockings, without exception, conform to the regulations. They are blue, made of nylon, and properly pulled up. Then it is the boys' turn. María Teresa has to bend down a little further to get a good look. She knows she has to pay attention: the boys realise their socks are not so visible, and so are more likely to break the rule. Take Calcagno, for example. His socks are blue, as they should be, but they are made of towelling rather than nylon. They are tennis socks, of a make showing a penguin dancing. María Teresa reprimands Calcagno, but does not punish him. She writes his name down in her register and warns him that the following day she will look to make sure his socks are the right kind. Calcagno promises to do as required, and the inspection continues. As she approaches Baragli, María Teresa has an uneasy feeling. She does not know exactly why, whether she will find him wearing red socks or what, but she feels a clear sense of foreboding. She looks down, and Baragli's socks are as they should be. Blue, made of nylon. But as he shows them to her, Baragli pulls his trouser legs up too far, revealing to María Teresa's close gaze not his shiny shoes or his regulation socks, but part of his leg, a strip of pale shin veined with dark lines of hair. He shows her this, makes sure she sees it; she has bent down so far she cannot now avoid the shocking detail of his bare skin. Baragli draws his first foot back, and immediately pushes the other one forward. María Teresa has still not recovered, a buzzing in her ears leaves her stunned, she can sense her cheeks growing heavier and turning pink. The other leg: Baragli stretches it out, and she is still bending forward: he is not going to show her his sock, his

57

scrupulous submission to the school rules. No, it is his leg, his shin, that Baragli is showing her, his male leg, his male hairs, a strip of skin exposed between the grey of the trouser turn-up and the blue of his sock. This time the trouser leg is raised even higher; more skin, more of his shinbone showing. María Teresa has turned red, and she knows it. She straightens up but still feels slightly giddy and confused. Baragli looks at her, frozen in the same attitude, with his sock and above it that skin, the skin with its blemishes. She can see every last detail, school regulations state that stockings must be blue and made of nylon, and Baragli has clearly fulfilled that requirement, María Teresa feels dizzy and has a buzzing sound in her ears, or perhaps it is the ringing sound that makes her feel dizzy; she does not feel well.

—Very good, Baragli. Get back in line.

She continues the inspection, head reeling. If any of the pupils made a glaring mistake, such as black or sky-blue stockings, she would not fail to notice it, but she is not sure if she would be able to spot anything more subtle, like Calcagno and his blue stockings made of towelling or cotton instead of nylon. She inspects the others as quickly as possible, wanting to get it over with: she does not feel at all well. She cannot be certain, but she thinks that beneath her blouse she has suddenly broken out into an untimely sweat. She is gradually feeling better, but only slowly. Her dizziness is slowly disappearing, and so is the buzzing noise. Her perspiration is drying off. She reaches Valenzuela, who is the last in the line. He is wearing grey socks, and when María Teresa reprimands him, her voice is no longer trembling.

—Your socks, Valenzuela.

—Yes, Miss.

—They're grey, Valenzuela.

—Yes, Miss.

—They are supposed to be blue, Valenzuela.

—Yes, Miss. The thing is, I had a problem.

—What problem, Valenzuela?

—The spin dryer at home broke, Miss.

—What happens in your home does not interest me, Valenzuela. Your socks are meant to be blue.

—Yes, Miss.

—Make sure they are, tomorrow.

—Yes, Miss.

—Not grey, blue.

—Yes, Miss.

—Tomorrow.

—Yes, Miss.

—Without fail.

María Teresa notes his name down on her register. She has already written: 'Calcagno: towelling socks.' Underneath she writes: 'Valenzuela: grey socks.'

Now comes the second part of the inspection. She is barely able to maintain her recently recovered composure, and still cannot understand what happened to her. Perhaps, she tells herself, it was sudden low pressure, one of those momentary blackouts that occur when someone bends down too quickly – or more correctly, when someone straightens up again too quickly after having bent down. María Teresa thinks that is what it must have been, her sugar levels must be low: she decides she will make herself a nice cup of lemon tea as soon as she gets back to the assistants' room.

These reflections help calm her, but the Head of Discipline

has called out for the second part of the inspection to begin, and that is enough to fluster her again. Checking the length of hair is also far easier with the girls: it is enough to cast a cursory overall glance to make sure they are wearing hairbands and slides, that their hair is tied neatly, that everything is as it should be. The boys' hair, however, demands much closer attention. The regulation states it must be no less than four centimetres above their shirt collar: this distance is usually measured by the width of two fingers of a normal adult hand. In many cases this is quite clear, because the nape of the boy's neck is completely shaven, and looks like a field burnt by fire. There can be no possible doubt. Nor is there any when locks of hair are so long they brush the shirt collar, or worse still, are actually touching it. In these cases also the offence is obvious. Between these two extremes, however, there is a fairly wide range of ambiguous cases, which are hard to resolve at a simple glance, and require the measurement of the distance between the hair and the boy's shirt collar. María Teresa is not happy about touching any of the boys' necks at the moment. She does not feel up to it. She thinks about it and does not want to, so she examines their haircuts with suppressed anxiety. She is genuinely relieved to find that Baragli's hair is clearly too long: she will not have to go any closer to him.

—Your hair needs cutting, Baragli.

—Yes, Miss.

She writes in her register: 'Baragli: haircut.' The same goes for Cascardo, Bosnic, Tapia and Zimenspitz. There are no dubious cases until she comes to Valenzuela. Valenzuela, the last in the line. The pupils are trying the same sly tricks as always: leaning their heads forwards, pulling the collar down behind, in an attempt to reach the four centimetres demanded by the regulation. Valenzuela is bound to try to do so, he is in fact wriggling around, but without success. María Teresa watches and calculates, hoping she will not have to intervene. But it is by no means certain she will be able to fit her two fingers in between his hairline and collar. Possibly yes, possibly no. And María Teresa cannot run that risk. If later on, or even during the inspection itself, the Head of Discipline or Señor Biasutto were to discover the infringement, as the assistant for third year class ten she would be responsible for the oversight. She is forced therefore to carry out the measurement as stipulated in the regulation, by placing two fingers on the back of Valenzuela's neck. The good thing about him being the tallest, and so the last in the line, is that none of the others will see what she is doing: no-one will be a direct witness. María Teresa goes up to Valenzuela. She will have to raise her hand a little to reach the back of his neck: it is imperative that when she does so it should not tremble, or that if it does, there is no way he can notice. She finally places two fingers on the pupil's nape. The skin is warm, and touching it feels strange. It is covered by a sort of down that is not exactly hair, although there is nothing else it could be, which makes the skin soft to the touch. Her two fingers: the index and the middle finger of her right hand, on Valenzuela's neck.

Her index finger is not touching the curls that cover Valenzuela's head like a wig, as if they were not part of him. María Teresa cannot hurry the procedure, quickly brush against his neck then remove her fingers as if she had come into contact with an electric cable or a pan full of boiling water. She must not let her anxiety show; she has to measure the gap calmly and make up her mind in her own time. So the contact between them lasts for one or two seconds, perhaps three. Only then does she withdraw her fingers from the nape of Valenzuela's neck. She is certain now that there is no need to sanction or warn the pupil.

—All right, Valenzuela. But don't let it grow any longer.

María Teresa is out of sorts for the rest of the day. At times she feels annoyed; at others distressed. She cannot wait to get home. As she travels in the metro, the darkness of the tunnel leaves her claustrophobic, as if there were no air. But although she was desperate to arrive home, once she is there she does not feel any better. Her mother's company is not much help: she spends hours on end watching television, and occasionally has the radio on at the same time. Bombarded with speculation rather than actual news, she has become an unrecognised expert in diplomacy and international negotiation. When nine o'clock comes round and it is time for supper, María Teresa has no appetite. She is not hungry at all. Her stomach churns, she feels revolted by the food. She stares at the tiny piece of chicken on her plate. To her eyes it looks like an extraordinary mess of torn flesh and indigestible bones: something difficult enough to contemplate, let alone eat. The mother says she should try anyway, arguing that a nauseous feeling often comes from not having tasted anything in a long while, and that the sickness will disappear as soon as she takes her first mouthful. Persuaded by the argument, María Teresa lifts a forkful of food to her mouth. She chews it for several minutes, but finds it hard to swallow. When she finally forces herself to do so, it is simply so that she can stop chewing. She leaves the rest of the chicken on her plate. Says she is going to bed.

—Without having a bath?

The idea of taking a bath repels her as much as eating. All she wants to do is to go to bed and close her eyes, to be sleeping already, to be asleep. She leaves the mother eating alone, shaking her head, while she undresses and takes refuge in her bed so that she can finally sleep. But she cannot. The very desire to plunge into sleep is what keeps her awake. She is unable to find sleep. At best, she reaches the threshold of falling asleep, as if she were rehearsing what it meant to sleep, but it is impossible for her to escape the waking world, and so she finds herself once more with her eyes wide open, the brightness filtering through the shutters hurting her eyes. Images flit through her mind: perhaps she really has fallen asleep and they are part of a dream, perhaps they are a trick her mind plays (a trick that will not let her sleep or which as soon as she does so, wakes her up again). These images jumble together Baragli's leg and the back of Valenzuela's neck; the two merge together to produce very odd combinations (for example, a nape with leg hair, or a shinbone with the down from the back of a neck, or two fingers stretching out to touch a leg). María Teresa appeals to the resource which ever since she was a little girl has helped her get to sleep peacefully and feel calm and protected; tonight though not even the rosary clutched in her hand brings her the peace she needs.

Weary from her insomnia, she decides to get up. She finds the mother sitting staring at the television, with all the lights off. The bluish light from the set gives the room a strange hazy glow.

—What are you watching?

—The news.

63

She sits in the other armchair and starts to watch as well. At first she cannot concentrate: her mind wanders to other things (for example, whether or not they will ever get a colour television), so that it takes her several minutes to realise that the strange quality of the news bulletin is not due, as she had thought, to her lack of sleep or the odd time she is watching it, but because there is no sound: wordless images, pure gesticulation.

—Don't you want to hear what they are saying?

—They always say the same.

—But if you're watching it, don't you want to hear what they're saying?

—When I want to listen, I switch on the radio.

On the screen a singer is clutching a microphone. He is singing with his eyes tight shut, but his mouth opens and closes in an exaggerated fashion. The lack of any sound makes it seem as though he is pulling faces. At the bottom of the screen is a strap-line that reads: 'Festival of Solidarity'. Every so often the camera cuts to views of small Argentinian flags being waved in the air. Then the news presenter comes on. He is not one of the star presenters – they are always on the main eight o'clock programme; in the middle of the night they use a less important figure, either a young person just starting out, or an old man about to take retirement. The next item is an interview with a black-bearded youth who is talking to the journalist, a thoughtful expression on his face.

—Who is he?

—I don't know; a singer, I think.

A sign appears at the foot of the screen: 'Julio Villa'.

—Ah, no. I thought it was Gianfranco Pagliaro, but it isn't.

The following images indicate that Julio Villa is a footballer. He is seen controlling a ball, then kicking it, wearing a shirt with sky-blue and white stripes.

—He plays for Argentina, doesn't he?

—It looks like it.

María Teresa dozes off in the armchair as the news programme ends and a film comes on (Argentinian cinema from the 1940s: the mother does not bother to increase the volume now either). María Teresa falls asleep without realizing it, overcome partly by tiredness, partly by boredom. The mother decides not to wake her up, in case moving her brings back her insomnia. Instead she fetches a blanket and covers her, taking care not to disturb her.

María Teresa wakes before sun-up. She has shooting pains in her neck and back. For the first time ever, she wishes she did not have to go to school. Of course she does not take the idea seriously; she knows she will go in, but this is the first day she has felt she would prefer not to go, that she would like to keep her distance from that world where she has to take the register, make sure the pupils line up properly, carry the text books, punish any infringements, stay permanently vigilant, avoid any lax behaviour, clean the blackboard, provide chalk, keep the school authorities informed, safeguard the school's proud tradition.

She is tired when she arrives at school, already wishing the day were over when it has barely begun. She can feel the lack of sleep in the way her eyes smart and her knees are creaking. Even the least insistent voices sound cavernous to her, as if they are echoing round a large room, and it is this echo that catches her attention more than what they are saying. When she takes the register for third year class ten, it is as though

65

she were hearing their surnames for the first time, and more than once she confuses 'Present' for 'Absent'. Fortunately her bad day is not made worse by any extra complications: Calcagno is wearing nylon socks, Valenzuela's are blue, Baragli, Bosnic, Cascardo, Tapia and Zimenspitz have had haircuts, and Valenzuela has taken the precaution of having his cut too. Capelán appears to have forgotten about Marré when they step apart in the quad. None of the teachers is absent: Miss Pesotto teaches Physics for the first two periods; the third and fourth are Latin with Mr Schulz; Mr Ilundain comes for the fifth lesson, which is Spanish, and the sixth is Geography, taught by Miss Carballo. María Teresa's tiredness helps her ignore Baragli and whatever he may be up to. Apart from verifying that he has had a haircut, she pays him no attention all afternoon. She carries out her inspection of the toilets from a sense of professional pride, reluctantly and with no real expectations, but discovers nothing new. She hardly sees Señor Biasutto all day, and this somehow unsettles her. The supervisor is holding constant meetings with the Head of Discipline and the Deputy Headmaster – perhaps in order to finalise the details of the patriotic celebrations soon to be held on 25 May, Independence Day, and so is hardly to be seen in the assistants' room or in the quads at break-time. Her exchanges with him do not go beyond a superficial greeting from afar; although she would like to, she has nothing to report. The day ends with the habitual singing of the 'Aurora' anthem while the Argentinian flag is lowered and folded in the central quad. The pupils, who usually do no more than murmur the words of patriotic songs, including the national anthem, now sing them with greater determination and much clearer diction. They can be heard singing out loud, rather than as usual leaving everything to the recorded soprano voice playing over the loudspeakers. They sing: 'High in the sky/ A warrior eagle/ Proudly rises/ In triumphant flight.'

For some reason María Teresa cannot even explain to herself, she completes her daily duties, but instead of heading for home at the first opportunity, finds excuses to stay on in the school. This is hard to understand, because today more than any other she had no desire to come to work, and would have preferred to have stayed in bed and do nothing; if she did come in it was out of her clear sense of duty and responsibility. She has done her work as required because she feels she has no other choice: it is part of the education she has received and the values she believes in. By now it is almost half-past six: the pupils of third year class ten have all left, the other class assistants as well, and she herself has finished everything she had to do – she has filed the attendance sheet, checked the teachers' signatures, made sure there was enough chalk in her classroom (which at ten past seven the next morning will be occupied by third year class five). She can go home whenever she wishes, she could be out in the street by now, she could be approaching the metro. Yet she stays on. Just as she had not wanted to come to school in the morning, now she has no wish to go home, and so she lingers. It does not occur to her to go somewhere else, anywhere else, apart from her own home. The idea does not even occur to her. Her range of choices is much simpler: she does not want to go home, so she remains at the school. Objectively, there is no reason for her still to be there, so she invents her own excuses to postpone the moment of departure. She checks registers she has already checked, reads the teachers' subject notes, files cards on punishments already carried out, puts pieces of chalk away in cardboard boxes, unrolls maps of Asia and Africa, only to roll them up again.

At ten to seven, she leaves the assistants' room. The school appears deserted. None of the third year forms have been kept back for the seventh hour, so there is absolutely no-one in the cloister. María Teresa is on the point of leaving: it could almost be said she is forcing herself to do so. She is going to leave, but wants to make one last detour. The shortest way out would take her towards the stairs at the end of the corridor, the ones next to the Headmaster's study. Without understanding why, today she decides to go down the staircase in the block furthest from her, the stairs by the library. To do so she has to cross the whole school: first her own quad, then past the tuck shop, the toilets, reach the other quad and cross that one too. Only then will she reach the staircase she wants.

The tuck shop is closed, and therefore shows what it really is: a kiosk made of corrugated iron. María Teresa comes to a halt outside it, as if she wants to inspect it. After a moment though she is more honest with herself, and looks behind her: nobody there. She looks in the opposite direction: no-one there either.

The silence inside the school is complete: there are not even any sounds in the distance. María Teresa lays one hand on the solid wood of the green swing doors. It would only take a slight push to open one side. She feels strangely calm, almost happy. She looks down at her hand on the door of the boys' toilet, and her hand transmits a certainty, a decision: she is going to open that door and go in.

68

6

The toilet door creaks as it swings open. During the day, when the cloisters are noisy with footsteps and conversations, the sound goes unnoticed. But now in the total silence the door emits a squeaking noise that sounds almost like an accusation. Already with one foot in the boys' toilet, María Teresa pokes her head inside. This is enough to make her senses spin. As sometimes happens in films, it is as if she has leapt into an unreal world: a world with different laws (gravity or child-free, for example), or a world in another time, where things are the same but have a different meaning. Despite this sudden transformation, she manages to take a very sensible precaution: instead of letting go the swing door after she has stepped inside, allowing it to swing back into position of its own accord, she keeps her hand on it, and eases it back alongside the other one, so that it does not protrude into the corridor and become visible to any prying eye.

In the same way as the quads, the toilet has glazed tiles up to a certain height, which María Teresa calculates must be about two metres; above that, the walls are painted as far as the distant ceilings. The only difference is that the colours in here are brighter: the tiles are ochre-coloured rather than dark green, the walls are painted a light yellow or white. There are four windows in the far wall. They are very high up, and are as firmly shut as all the other windows in the school. To open any of them you need one of the long metal poles with a special hook on the end which have to be fetched from the janitor's office (following written authorization by the Head of Discipline). María Teresa concludes that any smoke produced by clandestine smoking in the toilet could not drift out through them, and that they would not permit any welcome renewal of the air in the atmosphere by allowing a fresh breeze to enter. No opportunity for concealment there. But as she peers round her, she also concludes that the space is so big, the walls so distant and the ceiling so high, that if there were any smoke from black tobacco floating in the air, it would soon disperse and become diluted, and that this would greatly reduce any chance of her detecting it. She cannot decide which of these contradictory factors would be more important if the case arose. Even now that she is no longer sniffing the toilet from outside, but has boldly gone in, she is unable to say with any certainty just what smell predominates. It is definitely not that of black tobacco, either in the foreground or underneath the rest; but it does not seem clearly to be that of other toilets either – the smells of human waste, or even that of bleach used to clean it at the end of the day.

Against the far wall, but not directly opposite the entrance, there are five cubicles separated from one another by thin partitions. Each of these cubicles also has a door painted green. Everything about them is on a smaller scale: the doors do not come to the ground, and the walls do not reach the ceiling. They are enclosed areas, aimed at protecting a certain intimacy, but they are not entirely private, sealed off from one another. On the floor of each there is a white ceramic base. In the centre of this base is a hole, made doubly dark because it is surrounded by whiteness, and in the front part are two feet-shaped outlines that are ridged to prevent anyone slipping. María Teresa peers inside one of the cubicles: it is the first time she has seen any installation of this kind. She imagines what it must be like to use the toilet, and thinks it must be difficult to keep one's balance, hard not to topple backwards while bending down far enough to defecate without soiling the clothes around one's ankles. It seems to her very uncomfortable, and very demanding as regards directing one's aim. There is one way in which the boys' toilet is similar to the girls': the separation of these relatively private spaces. This confirms to her that everyone wishes to be completely alone to carry out certain functions. Apart from this, the girls' toilets are different because they have a toilet bowl in which to relieve themselves. Somewhat primitive ones it is true, and some of them lacking not only the lid but also the seat to sit on; still, they are much more modern and adequate than this other kind of toilet she has stumbled across. The boys must find it difficult to stay upright, and often miss the target. Completely lacking experience in the matter, María Teresa speculates about this in the abstract, and yet her deductions are correct. She proves this by peering inside another cubicle and finding a situation that is far from hygienic. This is not what is important to her, however; it is not what she is looking for. Struggling with her disgust, she searches for any trace of a cigarette butt trodden on the floor, or any sign of ashes. She carefully examines all round, but can find nothing. She looks inside every possible hiding place, but discovers no clues. Only two of the toilets are still dirty; the other three are fine, with no sign of being used. She steps into one of the clean ones. She feels the same strange mix of determination and doubt as she experienced when she entered the toilet in the first place. Once inside, she closes the door. She draws the bolt – the door is locked. She immediately calculates to what extent it offers her privacy. On the one hand, she is completely on her own, safe from anyone's prying eyes behind the locked cubicle door. On the other, she can see that the door only reaches down to her knees, and there are no roof or walls to contain any noises.

María Teresa tries out what the boys must have to do: she puts her feet on the ridged outlines and bends as if she were going to sit down, although the lack of a seat means she has to remain crouching in mid-air. She discovers that one possible way of gaining stability is by stretching her hands out to the side walls and pushing against them. All of a sudden she feels exhausted, and her legs begin to tremble. This could of course be due to her lack of sleep the previous night. The hole beneath her, or rather behind her, repels and attracts her at the same time. Of course it is a place for filth, and yet simply because of their shape these holes are mysterious: they have the form of mysteries. And María Teresa realises for the first time that boys are not like girls: their bodies are different. This is obvious, but she had never thought of it before. Any female – herself, for example – could crouch down in this complicated fashion and simultaneously perform the two necessary bodily functions. Males though (this much she does know) have a round floppy thing on their front (she has never seen one, but knows they do, because everybody knows that), and so she finds it impossible to explain how a boy could carry out both bodily necessities at the same time, aiming them both at the mystery of this hole where everything disappears.

Writing on the toilet walls in the National School of Buenos Aires is strictly forbidden. The walls seem clean in that respect. In other public toilets, for example, those in bars or bus stations, it is common to see all kinds of inscriptions, many of them extremely rude. María Teresa remembers one instance from her childhood, in a toilet at the Río Cuarto bus terminal, when she was going for six days' holiday in the trade union hotel at Villa Giardino. Their bus stopped for forty minutes in Río Cuarto so that they could have dinner. When María Teresa asked to use the toilet, her mother did not accompany her, merely pointing to a scuffed door and stuffing a damp wad of toilet paper into her pocket. María Teresa went in and sat down, and while she was silently relieving herself tried out her newfound skill of reading whole phrases. Most of the slogans scrawled on the wall were attacking General Onganía or supporting Boca Juniors football club. This was in 1969: in May there had been widespread political demonstrations in Córdoba, and in December Boca Juniors had won the national championship. In the midst of these phrases, though, she found another, smaller one, written in black ink that was perfectly visible to anyone looking for it. It simply read: 'I lick cunts', and beneath it was a telephone number. Even at that age, she knew what that word meant, although her mother never used it and she was forbidden to ever say it. It was a word men used. If

73

necessary, women had to refer to 'vagina', but it was better to avoid any reference to the topic at all. María Teresa was shocked to find this male word inside the women's toilet; she was worried it might be possible for a man to come in and find her there, with her knickers round her knees and her mother a long way off. She dried herself hurriedly, and rushed out of the toilet. She was impeded at every step by unforeseen obstacles, as if in a nightmare: the door would not open, she slipped on the floor, two big fat ladies prevented her leaving, she could not see her mother or brother.

Now, many years later, María Teresa remembers this episode, perhaps because she is a woman who has entered the boys' toilet. Of course she is there because she is the class assistant for third year form ten, and there is at least one pupil in the class, by the name of Baragli (but possibly more), who is smoking at school, which means he or they must be doing it in these toilets. Despite her association, the toilet walls here are impeccably clean. Nobody writes on them, there are no phrases or drawings to offend anyone, partly because the teaching at the school discourages that kind of thing, and partly because the glazed surface of the tiles makes any writing on them not only extremely difficult but means they can easily be erased by wiping them with a damp cloth.

On the wooden door, however, María Teresa can see scratches. At first sight these seem to be random cracks in the wood, splits caused simply by the passage of time. When she looks more closely, however, it becomes evident that these shapes are not fortuitous, that they have been made by a human hand, that these lines and curves once formed or were intended to form letters, and that these letters combined to make words. Looking more closely still, María Teresa realises they were dug into the wood, perhaps with a penknife or possibly, considering implements more directly related to the school environment, by the metal point of a compass, and not something simply produced by the contraction or wear and tear of the wood itself. Someone once wrote something on this door, and did not do so with ink or lead pencil. It was not done with anything that could be wiped off, but by a more drastic intervention, in the hope of making it indelible, like an engraving or carving: removing slivers of wood from the door, gouging them out, getting rid of them, in order to create words and phrases. In vain: the answer the school authorities came up with was to paint the doors again, smoothing over the surface of the incised wood and removing once and for all the existence of the slogan someone or other had written. The perfect solution: a coat or two of the same green paint, and the words disappeared forever.

And yet, as the years went by, there seems to have been a slow shift: the wood has absorbed the paint. The minute, unhurried incorporation of one substance into the pores of a different one, with each drop of paint assimilated by invisible cavities that insensibly draw them in. And so this toilet door, the door to the boys' toilet of the third year of the National School of Buenos Aires, has gradually recuperated part of what was written on it many years before. There is no longer any clear outline, but it is definitely still there. On close inspection, there is a slight depression, a difference of levels so minimal that it is easier to make it out with the fingers than with the eyes. That is why María Teresa touches, reaches out and feels the inside of the toilet door with her fingertips. Gradually she makes out shapes, as if she were blind and reading Braille. Shapes: a circle, a line going up and down, up and down, a tight curve that remains open at the top: shapes that form words. María Teresa tries to read, as if in Braille, the secret legend of the toilet door. She cannot understand the first word. She can follow some of the letters: an 'r', perhaps an 'f', but not the whole word. Then there is an 'o': a round, printed 'o'. Then —that is to say, beneath that – five letters she deciphers one by one, until she realises that together they make the word 'death'. Intrigued, María Teresa tries again with the first word, urging her tired fingers to feel the letters and understand. It is no use: in this part, the paint is still winning out over the wood. It has smoothed everything over to such an extent that the wood has not so far been able to overcome or reverse the process. The first word is still lost, incomprehensible. All she can read is 'or death'.

María Teresa moves away from the door and returns to the black hole of the toilet. She wants to find out if it is possible to see whatever may have fallen down there: used matches or half-smoked cigarettes. She presses her hands against the side walls as she did earlier, although this time she does not bend down or look towards the door.

She peers into the hole cautiously – the last thing she wants to do is lose her footing. She cannot see anything. Absolutely nothing. The hole disappears into utter blackness, as if evoking the rural origins of this kind of lavatory: not the ceramic base, nor the drain-pipe, the sewer, the city beyond, but the pit, the bottomless pit, the cesspit, the pit disappearing into darkness and the void of the earth. If, when they smoke, the pupils throw the matches, the ashes, and whatever is left of their cigarettes down there, there will be no way she can find any trace unless they make a mistake. One further reason for taking the course of action María Teresa has already chosen: to catch them red-handed.

She unbolts the door, opens it, and steps out of the cubicle. She is back again in the general area of the boys' toilet. Opposite her stand four quite small wash-basins, their age evident from the fact that they have two separate taps, one for cold water and the other for hot, instead of one mixer tap that can easily demonstrate the advantage of having warm water. In contrast to this anachronism, there is a modern touch: coloured soaps shaped like big eggs hang from metal hooks fixed in the wall above the basins. As wet hands rub them, these soaps gradually become thinner, until they disappear completely and reveal the secret of their metal skeleton. Until this happens, their plump rotundity yields to the boys' dirty fingers, their size slowly diminishing, but not their shape or colour. In all these respects, the boys' toilet is exactly the same as the girls'. So too in the pair of mirrors on the wall above the wash-basins. Since she is not very tall, María Teresa has to stand on tiptoe to see herself in one of them. She does so, and stares at her reflection. It is odd, it has been days or even weeks since she has stopped to look at herself in a mirror, and here she is doing it at the school where she works, in the boys' toilet of the school where she works. She stares at herself: the geometric fringe, permanent glasses, her round face, weak mouth, pallid complexion. She thinks

77

she looks as she always does: slightly insipid. She knows she is not attractive, and has always known it, and yet when she tries to think of herself as ugly, she is not convinced either. Ugly women can attract people – she knows this from that singer, Barbra Streisand, whom her brother likes. Not being pretty, María Teresa could have been ugly, but she is not. She considers herself again: she looks tired. She is paler than normal, and has violet-coloured patches beneath her eyes. Two lines at the corners of her mouth make her look severe. She smiles into the mirror: she wants to know if she looks better serious or smiling. She cannot make up her mind. When she is serious, she looks old-fashioned: not old but old-fashioned, like a woman from an earlier age, possibly a figure from a medieval painting. But when she smiles she shows her teeth, which are too big, and she thinks she looks stupid. An intermediate solution, neither one thing nor the other, is what lends her the usual insipid look.

Her feet are aching from standing so long on tiptoe: her toes and also the insteps, where she bends her feet upwards. María Teresa wonders whether she ought to wash her hands before she leaves: she has been inside the dirtiest cubicles, and has touched their doors and walls. She decides she will, and is about to do so, when the two ends of the toilet catch her attention. She has neglected them until now, even though they were the most visible section, the most obvious even from outside the toilet. The real feature of the boys' toilet, what most distinguishes it from the girls', is precisely what she now discovers: the row of urinals. At each end of the toilet are ranged five urinals, making ten altogether, although they are so similar on both sides, so perfectly symmetrical, that there could well be only five of them, opposite a big mirror faithfully reproducing them. María Teresa knows of course that boys do not sit down to urinate. Not simply because everyone knows that, but also because her mother was always scolding her brother at home for getting the toilet seat wet when he was too lazy to lift it. This is where boys behave differently from girls: they get out whatever it is they have dangling down in front and perform standing up what girls do sitting down in private. It is also here that boys openly reject all idea of privacy: they line up alongside one another, as if they were passersby pausing to look in a shop window, or on a metro platform waiting for the train to arrive. But it is not a window in front of them, or the empty metro tracks, it is the row of urinals, and they are standing there with their thing in their hands. María Teresa walks over to examine the five empty urinals where all this goes on, as if those actions withheld a secret that the place where they occurred could reveal. The urinals are tall, smooth and made of marble like headstones; they descend more or less from chest level to the floor. Thanks to some automatic device, they are flushed with water at regular intervals. They are drained by a handful of holes at the bottom. María Teresa bends forward to examine this area more closely; everything suggests the system is inadequate, or that the holes get blocked up too easily, because instead of being clear, there is a small swampy area around them. This is where traces of hours-old urine collect in a thick deposit that seems unlikely ever to drain away. The colour of this muck is equally thick: dense and muddy, a stagnant, motionless pool. Objects are floating or have sunk into

79

these microscopic lakes: scraps of paper, matted strands of hair, soft drink bottle tops, shavings from a sharpened pencil. But no cigarette ash, no butts. Nor is there any sign of those gold bands that come off cigarette packets when they are opened. María Teresa studies all this closely, without realizing she has crouched down once more. Just then the urinals flush. Trails of white water flow down the side of the vertical marble. She stares at these trails as if they were the slender waterfall in a stream that has not been fed by rain in many months. When this water reaches the bottom, it stirs the swampy mess a little without creating any bubbles, and the stale urine and whatever is floating in it sways a little. The colour of the tiny pond lightens several degrees. Its volume increases, although it does not threaten to overflow, and then very gradually subsides. This proves that some of what is collected there does go down the drain, that not everything is completely blocked.

From her crouching position, María Teresa is at an ideal height to see that halfway down, the white surface of the urinals changes colour. It becomes ochre-coloured, in some places almost brown, and the reason for this stain is obvious – this is the exact spot at which the boys' urine hits the back of the urinal. Again, it is different here to what happens with the girls: the boys' urine does not fall directly into the water, but is launched into the air as brazenly as those things they use to propel it. The shiny jet rushes out and hits the white slab of the urinal with great force, rather than merely sliding down it. Where it strikes the hardest, the white surface becomes stained, in a blotch with lines radiating out from the centre. The colour is not the same as urine, but reminds her of it. Without really thinking, but without any feeling of revulsion, María Teresa stretches out her first finger and touches the back of the urinal. She touches it, then starts to rub her finger to and fro. Perhaps she wants to test how permanent the stain is, to see if by rubbing hard she can make it disappear so that the slab comes up clean again. Or possibly it is the opposite, the reverse, and that what she wants to see is whether the liquid is so strong that if she rubs, it will come off on her fingertip.

María Teresa withdraws her finger, stares at it, sniffs it: there is no difference. Yet as she straightens up, she remembers the reason for her being here in the first place, before she was sidetracked in this way: she turns on the tap of the wash-basin next to her and starts to wash her hands. She rubs them in a circle on the smooth, soft soap where the boys usually rub their own hands. Then she rinses them, preferring to use cold water. She has nowhere to dry them, and so pulls out the small handkerchief she always keeps in her sleeve since she caught a cold. That gets rid of most of the wet, although she knows her hands will not be completely dry.

It is only now, as she is about to leave, that she suddenly wonders whether one of the cleaning staff might not be coming in to do their work. The cleaners are always very quiet: they wear blue overalls, no-one knows their names, and they are hardly ever seen during class-time. It is precisely at the end of the day that they fan out through the school with their big, bearded brushes to sweep the floors clean, remove any growing cobwebs, or sluice down the toilets with buckets of water.

María Teresa pokes her head out: no cleaners are in

sight. She leaves the toilet without hesitating. Now she is in the corridor: a public space. By the time she is out in the street, it has gone half-past seven. She is inclined to think it is not as cold as it was at mid-day, although this might be just her personal impression. She could not swear the temperature has not dropped at nightfall.

7

Neater than ever, the flowerbeds in Plaza de Mayo help give a clean and tidy look to the square as a whole. The time of year does not exactly help them flourish: it is towards the end of May, and the city's autumnal air is heavy and gloomy. Yet the rows of flowers are bright and colourful, and combine with the lively jets of water from the rubbish-free fountains, so that the sometimes tawdry, sometimes chaotic aspect of Buenos Aires' main square is lessened, and the sense of a harmonious landscape restored. This is the only place in Buenos Aires where great patriotic celebrations can be held. In a few days' time another anniversary of the May Revolution is to be commemorated. Gathered in large but orderly groups outside the Cabildo, where those historic events took place, are high dignitaries of the Church, stern members of the Armed Forces, chosen representatives of diverse social organizations (patriotic leagues, secret clubs, charities, philanthropic centres) as well as more loosely formed knots of the so-called general public. Above all, there are the perfectly-behaved lines of pupils from the National School of Buenos Aires.

This is a true exception to the rule: traditionally, the pupils march through the streets of Buenos Aires on 20 June, the date commemorating the passing away (in solitude and poverty) of Manuel Belgrano, national hero and former pupil at the school. It is on that day, the eve of winter in Argentina, that the current members of the school pour out onto the streets to march and show how unwaveringly they can keep their eyes to the front. They walk from the school building on calle Bolívar down to calle Moreno, and then to Avenida Belgrano. Here they turn and carry on to calle Defensa, where Santo Domingo church is situated. It is in the entrance to this solemn place of worship that the hero's remains have been laid to rest, surrounded by Greek effigies.

This year, however, there are exceptional circumstances, which warrant an exception being made: the pupils are to march through the streets a month earlier than usual, on 25 May rather than 20 June, or possibly 25 May as well as 20 June, and they are to do so in the opposite direction to usual: that is, leaving along Bolívar to calle Alsina, then down to Diagonal Julio Argentino Roca until they come out directly opposite the Cabildo in the middle of Plaza de Mayo. They are taking part in the official celebrations of another anniversary of the first cry of freedom in the entire South American continent. It is drizzling and windy, but no-one can complain about that, because history tells us that on the day itself, in other words on 25 May 1810, it also was raining, and nobody cared.

María Teresa's glasses are misted over. She wipes them every so often in order to be able to see properly. She is of course directly responsible for her third year class ten, but the instructions spelled out emphatically to all the assistants by Señor Biasutto are that they should all keep an eye on everyone. There is no fear of misconduct or any lack of discipline: inspired by their patriotic feelings, the pupils are unlikely to indulge in any unseemly behaviour. However, it is also clear that journalists will come to report on the event, and not only journalists from the local media (such as, for example, *Gente* magazine, the weekly *Somos* or *La Nación* newspaper founded in fact by Bartolomé Mitre, who also founded the school), but also journalists from abroad, from countries like France or Holland, who are in Argentina as correspondents. The pupils are instilled with a desire to expand their knowledge, but also to take pride in what they do know. They spend many hours learning English or French (those who study English from years one to four then do French in years five and six, and vice versa). Their usual teachers are Miss Soria and Mademoiselle Hourcade. When they heard there would be foreign journalists at the 25 May celebration, many of the pupils were excited at the idea that they might be able to practise their language skills with native speakers: French with French reporters, English with the English. There is obviously a very praiseworthy motive behind this, a desire similar to that of wanting to carry out experiments in chemistry, physics, or biology. But when the alert class assistants heard these comments, they passed them on to Señor Biasutto, who passed them on to the Head of Discipline, and he informed the Deputy Headmaster. The Deputy Headmaster went round each class in person to talk to the pupils and explain in simple but eloquent fashion that unfortunately they could not trust the foreign journalists to be completely honest; that the questions they asked might seem perfectly well-intentioned, but that the stories they later wrote for their own press back home could be just the opposite; that

85

any innocent declaration the pupils might make when they saw the little red light of a tape-recorder switched on in front of them could subsequently suffer (and there were more than enough reasons to fear this) grave distortions slyly intended to damage the image of Argentina in the eyes of the world. As a consequence, the school authorities gave strict instructions that there was to be absolutely no contact with representatives of the foreign press.

The school pupils line up stiffly facing the Cabildo. The assistants have to ensure that they all follow their instructions carefully. Some people in anoraks and carrying umbrellas come over:

— *Qu'est-ce que vous pensez de la guerre?*

None of the pupils respond. They smile, wave a hand, or pretend they did not hear, but none of them gives a reply. Soon it is time for the singing of the national anthem. For once, the musical accompaniment is not supplied by the scratchy sounds of a worn record, but by a proud rendition from the mounted grenadiers of the General San Martín regiment. The drizzle stops, but not the wind. Following this there is an impassioned speech by a dignitary wearing civilian clothes: dark grey suit with matching tie under a black raincoat glistening from the rain. His voice echoes round the square. Emotional reactions abound.

María Teresa wipes her glasses with a small orange cloth, but cannot make them as clear as she would like. She puts them back on but still sees everything through a mist. She peers through it at the pupils of third year class ten. It is odd to see them like this, lined up as usual in their uniforms and with expressionless faces, but outside school, outside the quads and classrooms, in the open air, at the mercy of the elements. Her mind wanders again, until a shout from the crowd of 'Long live Argentina!' snaps her out of it.

The event draws to a close and the crowd starts to disperse. The clouds do not lift, but the sky seems lighter. María Teresa notices Señor Biasutto coming towards her. He looks so determined she thinks he must want to say something, but in the end he does not speak. He stays close by her, merely raising an eyebrow or wrinkling his forehead as if to communicate that everything is in order. She smiles faintly to show that she agrees.

The school pupils stay in rows, silent witnesses to the slow dispersal of men wearing purple, those in olive-green caps, the ladies with their smart headscarves, the crowd with their little plastic flags. Only when they have all gone are the pupils told to march off in formation back to school. They have to repeat to themselves the military rhythm 'left-right, left-right' (to think but not say it, like the one-two-three, one-two-three of people learning to dance, trying out new steps on the polished floor), so that they are all perfectly in step with each other.

When they reach the front stairs, the assistants watch the pupils going into school. They enter class by class. At the doorway, Señor Biasutto once again comes over to María Teresa. It seems so clear there is something he wants to say to her that she turns towards him, ready to listen. Instead, he lowers his gaze, wrings his hands, and the thin line of his moustache trembles. He does not say anything. María Teresa thinks she must have upset him, and so turns back to survey the pupils, at the moment when her class is starting to climb the grey steps.

That evening she discovers that being out in the wind and

autumn drizzle has made her cold worse. She spends the weekend in bed, with occasional bouts of fever. She coughs and sneezes, her throat aches, and her continually blocked nose makes her feel sleepy. Meanwhile in the living-room the mother spends her time with the television and the radio; for days now she has adopted the language of nautical technology. Two postcards arrive from Francisco, the two of them together but in different envelopes. He must have posted them at a few days' difference: one on a Thursday, for example, and the other the following Tuesday, or one on a Monday and the other a week later; but the Azul post office, or the postal service on the Azul base, apparently collects quantities of mail before sending the letters out all together to their respective destinations, so that the exact moment they were written becomes irrelevant, as they are all dispatched on one single day.

The two postcards show the same image of the statue of General San Martín in the main square at Azul. Even so, they are not identical, because in one of them the colours are much duller, as though the original photograph was taken on a cloudy day (that, however, is not the real reason: this postcard, but not the other one, must have suffered from being exposed to the sun for a long time while on display in a rarely-changed shop window, and it is well-known that over time this kind of exposure bleaches out colour).

On the back of the first card, Francisco has written his name and surname. On the other, the one he posted several days later but which arrived at the same time, he wrote only his first name. María Teresa keeps her brother's cards in the bedside table drawer, among religious pictures and childhood family photographs. During the days she is recuperating, she repeatedly takes them out and reads them over and over, as though they were long letters with lengthy anecdotes. She cries and prays, sometimes for peace, at others for victory, but always for her brother. The rest of the time she dozes in bed, and if she feels better she gets up to keep the mother company. They watch television together and share sporadic comments.

—What can I say, Marita? I've never ever liked the sea.

In the evening they play rummy. The mother always wins. She does so because she is better at guessing, but also because she has an extraordinary memory for the cards that have already gone. The radio and television are still there in the background: the television is showing a lengthy fund-raising programme, full of tearful faces and offers of jewellery (just like the ladies of the city of Mendoza who entered into history thanks to their donations to General San Martín's heroic venture across the Andes to liberate Chile); on the radio they are alternating songs in Spanish and interviews with prominent figures from Argentinian society, who talk with great emotion about heroism and the cold weather.

That night the telephone rings. It is unusual for this to happen: neither María Teresa nor the mother have many friends. Francisco does, but he is not there, and so these days almost nobody calls. The ringing of the telephone startles them.

—Who could that be?

The mother shrugs her shoulders.

—You get it, Marita.

They behave as though there were something to fear in

89

MARTÍN KOHAN

a telephone call. Before she picks up the receiver, María Teresa smooths her hair with both hands. The mother looks expectantly at her. María Teresa is anxious, but as soon as she hears the familiar voice over the buzzing at the other end, her expression changes to a smile: it is Francisco calling from the south. He has managed to find some tokens to make the long-distance call, but they have to make the most of the short time they have. The brother says he is fine, no longer in Azul but in Bahía Blanca, and is fine; he does not want to talk about himself, but to ask after them, the mother and sister; he has nothing to say about his new life: they should tell him their news. So María Teresa informs him a little about what they are seeing on television, and hearing on the radio; the surprise call has made her nervous and she mixes things up, gets confused. All at once, almost without saying goodbye, she hands the telephone to the mother. The mother uses the rest of the time, until she hears a click and then the busy tone, to give him dozens of recommendations: to keep warm, eat properly, avoid catching a chill, about his friends, smoking, draughty rooms at night, about authority and obedience, the benefits of getting a good night's sleep. While the mother is speaking she does not cry, not even when the call finishes and she has to hang up. In fact, these days she hardly sheds any tears, sometimes almost none at all, much less anyway than when Francisco was in Villa Martelli. What she has done is become an expert in naval terms, talking of nautical miles and knots, words she never used before.

These two days of rest allow María Teresa to recover from her illness, or rather to prevent it, if, properly speaking, it could be said she was never really ill. On Monday she returns to school as good as new, and in fact with an energy she has not felt for some time. She feels more confident, more determined to take the initiative.

—Don't lean there, Capelán. Don't hang, it's not a clothes hanger. Step apart, that's all.

She has thought deep and hard about her method of investigation in the boys' toilet. She has seen her mistake: going into the cubicles after hours demonstrated it clearly to her. Her error was to concentrate on the boys' toilet during the breaks between lessons, in the belief that this would be when anyone wanting to smoke in secret at the school would do so. But now that she has seen the empty toilet for herself, the quiet, forlorn toilet, she understands this was the wrong approach. If anyone, Baragli for example, or Baragli and others, is smoking at school, as she has strongly suspected ever since her sensitive nose alerted her, he or they must do it in the toilet, because there is no other possible place, but not as she thought during the breaks, because at that time lots of pupils are going in and out and would notice something, and anyone breaking the rules would not want so many possible witnesses. Anyone smoking in the toilet, Baragli for example, or whoever else it might be, must be doing it during classes, when cloisters and toilets are deserted, or almost so, when the teachers are busy in the classrooms and the assistants are dealing with administrative duties in their own rooms on each floor. This must be when those pupils raise their hands, and the teacher sees them and asks what question they have, and they say no, no questions, just an urgent need to go to the toilet. The teachers are not keen on permitting pupils to leave classes, and some of them even refuse in all cases; others, however, do occasionally give permission for them to go to the toilet, and the pupils leave the room.

After making this discovery, María Teresa completely changes her strategy. She does not spy on the toilets during the breaks: there is no need. Instead, sure that she is right, she takes a crucial decision. One afternoon, at the end of the first break, in other words during the third period, she slips unnoticed out of the assistants' room, glides through the empty cloister, and creeps secretly into the boys' toilet. She is already familiar with the place, but the situation now is very different: this time it is likely (and indeed for her, certain) that a boy will come in. This is why she hastily hides in one of the cubicles, bolts the door, and waits. As the minutes go by, she finds that instead of becoming calmer, as usually happens, she grows more nervous. Her increasing anxiety is because at any moment she expects to hear the creak of the swing doors at the toilet entrance, and to have her investigative efforts finally come to fruition. A pupil will come in and María Teresa, who is an assistant but also a guardian of the school's reputation, will discover whether he is behaving properly, without him being aware of it.

The first time she keeps watch in a cubicle, no-one comes in, but that does not discourage her. She is well aware that this is simply a first test; she never imagined there would be a constant flow of pupils during class time, nor that the defiant act of smoking there would be a permanent one. What she is after is the exception rather than the rule (because what she wants to confirm is nothing less than the rule being broken). This requires not only the virtue of patience but the ability not to give up. Aware of this, she returns to the same spot at later times on subsequent days. It becomes a kind of habit with her. Her insistence begins to bear fruit, even though of a modest kind. She has not yet managed to catch any smoker *in flagrante*; but from her hidden lookout post she is able to check on the way the boys use the toilet. Finally one day she hears someone come in. She hears the door swing open and then shut, and the boy's footsteps as he enters the toilet. There are no more than two or three steps, enough to take him from the door to the closest urinal. María Teresa presses herself against the cubicle wall, and tries to breathe more quietly. She can hear and sense everything: the pupil has come to a halt in front of the urinals she knows so well. His belt is loosened, the zip on his trousers undone. Now he must be using his fingers to get out that thing he has; he must be holding it in his hand. In order not to give herself away, she scarcely draws breath, although she somehow realises this is not the only reason why she feels she cannot get enough air. She can now clearly make out the liquid sound of urine gushing out, splashing against the white surface and snaking its way down to the bottom drain. When the noise stops, she remembers her father telling her brother when they were little to make sure he shook his thing afterwards so that there would be no drops in his trousers. That must be what the boy is doing now: gently hitting or waving whatever it is boys have dangling down in front of them. Without knowing why, María Teresa closes her eyes, as though by not seeing she is more likely not to be seen. After that the pupil doubtless puts his thing away, folding it or stuffing it inside his underpants, the zip is done up again, the loosened belt is tightened once more, the boy does not wash his hands as hygiene requires, but simply takes the three steps back the way he came, pushes open the swing door, and leaves.

María Teresa discovers that her hands and legs are trembling. She has also perspired a little, even though the weather is so cold. She thinks this must be from a fear that, trying to catch the boys out, she herself is caught instead; but she imagines that as the days go by she will feel more secure in her hiding place. True enough, the pupils come and go without suspecting her presence in any way. They enter, do what they have to do, and leave, without once looking round the toilet. Only anyone sneaking in to smoke might take precautions, but these would doubtless consist in checking that there was nobody *close* to the toilet, rather than being worried that there was someone *inside* it. And anyway, until now not a single boy has come to the toilet to smoke.

Nobody, not even Señor Biasutto, has noticed María Teresa's absences from the assistants' room, because it is normal that they come and go to perform their duties. The cloisters are so quiet during classes that she is increasingly unconcerned about entering and leaving the boys' toilet. She is no longer worried that anyone could catch her unawares. Once she is inside and has locked herself in one of the cubicles, she feels completely safe. She still gets nervous, especially when a boy enters the toilet, but repetition and habit mean that her confidence grows steadily, to the extent that she could be said to be enjoying doing what she is doing. She justifies herself briefly: she is carrying out her duties as an assistant to the full, and the day when she finally reaps the rewards for all her effort by uncovering the pupils smoking at school, she will be congratulated by her colleagues, and in particular by Señor Biasutto.

Much of her time is taken up with other tasks, such as taking the register for third year class ten, making sure they line up properly in the quad, telling them to stand by their desks because their teacher is about to enter the room. While doing all this she feels slightly anxious: she wants the class to begin so that she can go off and hide in the boys' toilet. She anticipates this moment even in the morning, when she is at home and has to leave to face another day's work at school. Many things will happen during the day, some of them interesting but perhaps most of them neither here nor there; yet above all María Teresa longs increasingly for the moment when she can enter and crouch (although not literally) in the boys' toilet. These minutes of waiting and watching hidden in a cubicle soon become the centre of gravity of her days at school. Anything that might happen prior to this is a kind of prelude: the tedious wait for what is truly important. And whatever takes place afterwards, in what remains of the day once she does not have to go into the boys' toilet, seems to her no more than an epilogue: the epilogue to something that has already occurred and which therefore can add nothing.

In her view, the only disadvantage to this is that her contact with Señor Biasutto is considerably diminished. As she is less often in the assistants' room, where the supervisor most often interacts with his team, she has fewer opportunities to exchange any words with him beyond the usual polite greetings. However, she is convinced that her constant watch over the toilet ought to be her chief concern at this time, even as regards her relationship with Señor Biasutto, because the successful outcome of her permanent vigilance will in the end provide a reason for him to appreciate her all the more. Yet another reason for her to feel that everything else that might happen to her is of secondary importance. It is only when she is hidden in the boys' toilet that María Teresa feels useful and at peace with herself.

8

The pupils who smoke in the toilets, Baragli and whoever else, Baragli or whoever else, must do so in the shelter of the cubicles. It is difficult, if not impossible, for them to try to light a cigarette at the urinals. Any smoke from there would not merely be smelled but clearly seen by anyone looking from outside. Some of the boys enter to wash their faces: they lean over the wash-basins, cup water in their hands to splash their eyes and cheeks with the obvious intention (because it is not hot) of driving away sleep and returning more alert to their class.

Several days go by before a pupil comes in and enters one of the cubicles. Whoever it is chooses precisely the one next to María Teresa's. At first, she strains to listen for the sounds she is hoping to hear: a match being struck, the glow of a light, the first puff on the cigarette, the first curl of smoke climbing towards the high ceiling. Soon however she realises that this is not what has brought the pupil there, but the more usual reason, and so she immediately changes her attitude, striving to ignore anything she might, even without meaning to, smell or hear, and simply listens to check whether the boy washes his hands with soap before returning to his classroom. He does.

It is odd what happens to her: it is clear that her hopes of finding the clandestine smokers at school depend on boys going into the cubicles, and not simply to the urinal. And yet she feels a slight sense of disappointment whenever a pupil comes into the toilet to enter a cubicle rather than stand in front of a urinal. She explains this to herself in the following manner: every boy who uses a cubicle and then does not smoke (in other words, all of them so far) brings a very unfortunate consequence: she has to suffer the filthy smell and equally filthy noise of their straining efforts (the same, or similar, as with the one who came into the toilet to be sick). Those who are coming in to urinate, however, by definition cancel out any possibility they are going to smoke and therefore be discovered by her, and this gives her a certain rather vague and unconfessed pleasure. María Teresa has already noticed the strange tingling sensation in her body the moment the boys start to urinate. She quickly attributes this to the fact that hearing someone else do so arouses her own wish to imitate them, in the same way as seeing somebody else yawn makes one want to yawn as well, or that when everyone is laughing one also starts to laugh, without knowing why. Yet one day she herself feels a terrible need to urinate, and the sensation is very different. María Teresa does not consider the difference. As usual, she is witnessing one of the boys relieving himself (partly directly aware of it, partly intuiting it) when she is suddenly overcome by her own urge. She is even worried she might do it in her knickers. Desperately she controls herself until the pupil leaves, squeezing her legs together and trying to think of something else. To make matters worse, the boy takes his time leaving: he is one of the painstaking ones, who even washes his hands. When he finally goes, María

Teresa tells herself she ought to get out at once and hurry to the staff toilet. It is only then that the most obvious thing strikes her: she is already in a toilet, and that if she wants to relieve herself she is in the most convenient place for doing so. Of course she does not, as she would have liked, have a toilet bowl to sit on, or any paper to wipe herself with properly. But for good or ill she is in a toilet; there is no reason to risk being found out by leaving in too great a hurry. She looks down at the ceramic base, and makes her mind up: she will urinate here, in the boys' toilet. The idea appeals to her, and she smiles, in her opinion because she has found a solution to her problem so quickly.

She finds she has to hitch her long plaid skirt up a little. Then she pulls her knickers down almost to her knees, but is still worried she may get them wet because of the unusual position. She yanks them down still further, almost to her ankles, but discovers that the danger of wetting or splashing them is even greater. After much hesitation, she makes up her mind and takes her knickers off altogether. She crumples them into a ball, and clasps them in her right fist like a bunch of flowers after the flowers have gone. The knickers are pink and lacy. She has never touched or seen her own underclothes this way before. All this makes her so nervous she cannot perform, although she is still as desperate as ever. She cannot use the trick of making the long hissing sound her younger brother taught her when they were little, because her main aim in the boys' toilet is not to make any noise. All she can do is wait.

Finally the wee comes, falling like a drop of dew off a leaf where it has been hanging for hours, as if falling by its own weight. María Teresa is pleased at what she has

99

done, apparently because she felt such a great need to do it. She is unused to this feeling of being dressed but not having any underwear on, with a skirt but no knickers. She experiences it for what it is, another way of being naked, more intense in some ways than the only other kind of nakedness she knows, that of taking a bath or shower at home. She raises the folds of her tartan skirt a little higher, and, slightly surprised at herself, peers downwards. She has never done this before, and never thought she would be capable of it: to watch herself weeing. An opaque yellow trickle is coming from her most intimate region. Seeing everything like this, she is suddenly aware of the fact that she is using those secret parts here, in the boys' toilet. María Teresa prevents the stream of urine falling straight into the black hole, because that would cause more noise and might attract attention. Instead she twists her body a little to one side, so that her wee hits the curved side of the white base and makes only a soft, trickling sound. When she has finished, she stays for a few moments in the same position: bending over with knickers in hand. Then she quickly dries between her legs with a bit of paper she always keeps with her, adjusts her clothing, sees what time it is and realises she has to leave the toilet, to get away, and rushes out. The cloister she emerges into is empty; the tuck shop that will be so busy at break-time is empty and locked.

As she leaves, she is jubilant. She does not really understand why. After all, she has not managed to catch any of the school's clandestine smokers, which is her only objective in all this. She has not yet succeeded, but she is jubilant. She explains it to herself as being because she is sure that sooner or later she will do so. For now, she is content. Throughout these days, although the general atmosphere around her is one of great concern, she herself feels at ease. She arrives at school in a good mood, knowing there is a whole day of work as an assistant ahead of her, and leaves in an equally bright mood, knowing she will be back the next day. It is true that at night she cannot sleep properly, and that quite often she wakes up with a start or in tears due to a nightmare whose details she is unable to recall. But she always gets up in a cheerful frame of mind, even if she feels tired from the lack of sleep, and when it is time to leave for work, she does so in good spirits.

Her father always said that life was a question of habit. As the days go by, it has become such a habit for her to hide and keep watch in the boys' toilet that she has even got into the habit of weeing there every time. She no longer waits as she did at first to have a need to do so. She simply does it, and finds she enjoys it. Sometimes she does not even feel any urgency, apart from the tingling sensation she still gets whenever a boy comes into the toilet, but that is not strictly speaking a need to relieve herself. She goes into a cubicle and takes her knickers off, as if she were desperate, even though she rarely is. Often she manages only a few drops, out of a sense of obligation, but sometimes absolutely nothing comes; she remains completely dry. She is never dismayed by this inability to perform, nor does it make her question herself. By now it has become a way to spend her time at school: it is just another part of the routine. Nor is she upset by the fact that despite all her efforts, she has not yet been able to discover anyone to punish. The days go by, and still no-one has entered the boys' toilet to smoke in secret. She realises that some of the boys come in for nothing, which is an infringement too, but not one that interests her. They enter the toilet and do nothing, or at most urinate briefly, as a cover-up, because what they really wanted was to get out of the class for a while to have a breather. María Teresa can sense what they are up to: they come in, walk up and down in front of the urinals, and finally go up to one in a bored fashion. They unzip their trousers, reach in and pull out their thing, squeeze out a thin stream or two, shake themselves, put it away, do the zip up again, wash their hands: those who are there simply to waste time never seem to forget to wash their hands.

One afternoon a pupil enters the toilet and goes into the second cubicle. He has not come to smoke, and does not do so. He does not give off the smell of a match being struck or of tobacco being consumed. And yet there is not the smell of the more disgusting emptying of his bowels either. María Teresa is so close to him she knows he has undone his trousers, but all she can be certain of is her intuition that the boy's thing is already out. She cannot hear him either peeing or getting rid of his bodily waste. What she can hear, with great clarity, is the boy's breathing, and this pleases María Teresa. There is neither a pleasant nor an unpleasant smell, and the only sound is of his lungs filling and emptying. All of a sudden however, she does smell something, which seems to her not dissimilar to that of the cleaning bleach.

The pupil takes some of the toilet paper, crumples it, and throws it into the black hole. He pulls the chain (the toilets are so antiquated they still have a chain, not a handle or button). He does his zip up and leaves. María Teresa is not interested in what he did, or whether in fact he did anything at all. The important thing is that he did not smoke, that he did not light a cigarette or blow clouds of smoke into the air. In fact, far from being upset, she is pleased to have witnessed from her secret hiding-place – pressed up as ever against the thin partition – this unknown pupil's own secret. She is, however, rather intrigued by the episode, and several questions go through her mind: who was it, what did he do, why did he come, what was he there for? She ponders these questions without the need to find any definite answers. She respects his secret, perhaps sensing that this means her own secret is safe too.

On the days when there are written tests, the number of pupils coming into the toilet diminishes considerably. Not even the most lenient teachers would permit a pupil to leave the room during a test: it is obvious they could take the opportunity to quickly consult one of those bits of paper scrawled with formulas and other answers that they usually hide in their pockets or their stocking elastic. Leaving the classroom during exam hours is quite simply impossible. If any of the boys is truly desperate, and really cannot wait, or if any of the girls tacitly alludes to that female condition that has to be discreetly dealt with, then the solution is simple: the pupil concerned may go to the toilet, but first they have to hand in their exam paper with the work they have managed to do so far, and that is what they will be marked on. If, for example, they have got halfway through the test, answering say two out of four questions, or solving two out of four equations, and have done so without making any mistakes, they will get five out of ten. The pass mark is seven. The teachers often enthusiastically comment to the assistants or among themselves how quickly the pupils' need to go to the toilet vanishes when they are reminded of this rule.

—You see? It wasn't *that* urgent after all.

However, there are subjects which for some reason are seen as less strict, even if failure in them means the pupils have to sit an exam at the end of the year in December, or in March, and possibly cease to be a regular attender at the school (no-one is allowed to repeat a year at the National School of Buenos Aires: instead, they are dispatched to another school, one of the ordinary ones, and that diaspora is the mark of their failure). These subjects are, for example, art or music, and occasionally Spanish as well (not the language part, but literature). The hours spent daubing on bits of card, listening to arias or reciting couplets are not viewed as strictly as the physics, maths, or history lessons (or Spanish when it comes to subordinate adverbial clauses or the correlation of verbs). During these lessons, dedicated, let's say, to the notion of perspective or to the composition of a philharmonic orchestra compared to a symphonic one, it is far more likely for the pupils to ask to leave the room to go to the toilet, and for the teachers to give permission. María Teresa is well aware of this: she knows that is what happens, and takes it into account. On days when there are written tests, it is more probable she will be keeping watch and no pupil will come in for any reason (not even to smoke). But when one or other of the third year forms has art or music, then there is a greater chance that the second-floor toilet will receive visitors.

It is not unimportant for María Teresa that the form having an art or music lesson is third year class ten, the one she is in charge of. When that happens, she always remembers it. Because the inexorable price to pay for the secrecy of keeping watch in the boys' toilet is that whereas, on the one hand, it betrays some aspects of well-preserved privacy, on the other, it never reveals the identity of the pupil in question. Only when what María Teresa knows is bound to happen finally occurs will she be able to break the rule of anonymity, making public both her own presence in the toilet and her lengthy spying.

Until that happens, she cannot give anything away, and it has not yet happened. The pupils come in and she is aware of them, in fact she is a witness to their most private functions, she can sense their relieved smiles, the way in which they handle themselves, but that does not mean she has a precise idea of who they are. When third year class ten has a music or art lesson, or when they have Spanish and Mr Ilundain decides to spend it giving an improvised reading of *La Celestina*, she knows, waiting silently in her cubicle, that any pupils entering the toilet will most probably be from her class, in other words the ones she knows best and can put a name to. She may not know exactly who it is, but she can be more or less sure that it will be one of those whom she sees every day lining up in the quad, sitting at their desks, bending over to pack away their things, doing up their jackets as they stand up. She knows it could be Barrella or Capelán or Iturriaga or Valenzuela, that the pupil might be Baragli or Valentinis, Kaplan or Rubio. Or one of the other boys in the class. And she secretly prefers this. Yes, she definitely prefers it. She tells herself this is because she has no proof that in any of the other third year classes at school in the afternoon (third year form eight, six, nine, seven or eleven) there may be pupils who smoke on the sly in the toilet. She is certain, on the other hand, that there are some in third year class ten, or that there is at least one, Baragli by name, who does or has done so. She therefore waits with great anticipation, and often even anxiety, for her class to have these lessons, and her stealthy wait is all the more enjoyable.

On Fridays, for example, third year class ten has a double period of art, with no break in the middle. María Teresa looks forward to this from the morning when she is still at home, clearing away the breakfast dishes or laying the table for lunch, while the mother cooks and is busy counting aircraft. She looks forward to going into the boys' toilet, hiding in the cubicle, waiting for a boy to come in so that she can finally catch him. She is excited by the thought, and when the time finally arrives, she enjoys it. She is not disappointed that in the end none of the pupils who has come into the toilet until now has tried to smoke, and so brought her patient pursuit to a happy conclusion.

For the same reason, she is put out and annoyed when third year class ten has art but she is unable to follow the routine of going and hiding in the toilet. She was expecting to be able to, and is impatient for the moment to arrive. But in the previous break, when the time to go is near and her sense of anticipation is increasing with every minute, she is summoned by Miss Perotti, the art teacher. She explains that they will not be going up to the artroom because she is giving a theory class, and that since she wants to show some slides she needs María Teresa's help with the projector. She cannot work it herself, she explains, because she will have to stand by the screen to use her pointer to show the parts of the works the pupils need to pay particular attention to. Nor can she ask a pupil to do it, because if he or she were busy showing the slides they would be sure to concentrate less on the aesthetic appreciation of the works on display. She would therefore like María Teresa, as class assistant, to stay in the room and help her with the slides. Unable to refuse, María Teresa accepts without hesitation. At any other time, the request would not have bothered her in the slightest. Every assistant is expected to collaborate fully with the teachers. And it is not that she will not carry out the task, still less refuse from the outset, but to know for certain that there will be a double period of art for third year class ten and that the pupils, as they always do in these more lenient lessons, will ask permission to go to the toilet, and that she, María Teresa, will not be there, upsets her so much she can barely hide her disappointment.

This situation could be enough to spoil her entire day. Some things manage to ruin a day even if they are only a tiny part of the greater scheme of things. María Teresa is annoyed because she feels her whole Friday will be wasted. Fortunately for her, and to compensate for the disappointment or to make up for it altogether, the request from Miss Perotti is not the only thing that happens during the first break. Señor Biasutto, her supervisor, comes up and leads her off to a corner of the quad. He puts his heavy hand on her forearm to guide her there. His pencil moustache twists in a forced smile. Señor Biasutto tells María Teresa that he found their conversation of the other day extremely interesting. María Teresa manages to think, but not to say, that she found it very interesting too. She does not succeed in saying so because Señor Biasutto quickly adds that he would be delighted to renew their conversation, and even to extend it in a more relaxed atmosphere. María Teresa flushes, but concurs. Señor Biasutto completes the proposal by suggesting that one day they might go and have a coffee together after school in a nearby bar. María Teresa is embarrassed to the point she can feel her cheeks reddening, and is so bewildered she does not even manage to say yes. Despite that, it is plain she is accepting his invitation, and Señor Biasutto understands this.

9

Cándido López was a soldier in the Argentinian army during the war with Paraguay. That war, also known as the War of the Triple Alliance, lasted for five years from 1865 to 1870. Three countries (Argentina, Uruguay and Brazil) united to obliterate a fourth (Paraguay). Many people have glimpsed the hidden hand of Great Britain in the original declaration of hostilities. This historical episode has always been of particular interest to the National School of Buenos Aires, because it was Don Bartolomé Mitre, the school's founder (more properly in this instance, General Mitre), who declared war and led the troops for the first three years. Despite underestimating the length of time the campaign would last, Bartolomé Mitre was in command of the nation's armies in those distant regions with such sonorous names: Curupaití, Tuyutí, Tacuarí. Although Mitre prophesied he would be entering the Paraguayan capital Asunción within three months, and that three years later he left the presidency still without having done so, this inaccurate prophecy in no way tarnishes the reputation of the patriot who wrote the history of Argentina's greatest national heroes, founded the newspaper with the longest tradition and prestige in the entire country, as well as its most important school, translated Dante's *Divina Comedia* with considerable accuracy, and achieved the permanent unification of the national territory. On close consideration, it could be said that even the War of Paraguay was won in the end, and that victory can be counted among General Mitre's laurels, as well as being one of the military triumphs of the Argentinian nation, whose flag, it is worth recalling, has proudly emerged undefeated from every challenge.

As she is setting up the projector, María Teresa listens to the teacher. The apparatus casts a yellow light that reminds her of the one in the carriages on the Line A metro: a light that seems to come from another age. There is also a rush of warm air, like someone breathing next to her. María Teresa slots the slides into the carousel. She checks each one to make sure they are in the right order and the right way up, so that none of them appears upside down and ridiculous. She also checks that no pupil has tried the trick they sometimes pull, slipping in a slide that has nothing to do with the topic the lesson is meant to illustrate. So, for example, there may be a series of Ionic and Doric columns, or of Assyrian bas-reliefs, and then suddenly, without justification or warning, there is the shock of a family snapshot: two children with their parents smiling at the camera with the sea and the beaches of Miramar in the background. And that would not be the worst possibility. Apparently once, years earlier, when a history master was illustrating his lesson with coloured slides of Napoleon Bonaparte, all at once, between an imposing picture of the Great Corsican mounted on a white horse and another of his coronation as emperor in Notre Dame cathedral, there appeared, to general laughter, the unlikely sight of a naked woman (an American actress by the name of Raquel Welch) showing off her breasts, her hair blowing in the wind.

María Teresa does not want anything of the sort to happen now. She checks carefully: the only slides in the carousel are the twenty-four reproductions of Cándido López's paintings of the War of Paraguay. The projector has been set up on the second desk in the third row in the middle of the room, pointing towards the screen that Miss Perotti has pulled down over the blackboard. In order to work the projector, María Teresa has had to take the place of one of the pupils (Rubio, who is sitting at Iturriaga's desk, because he is absent). She has never sat here before, and so has never seen things from the pupils' point of view. The teacher's platform seems higher, the blackboards seem to fill the whole front wall, the door and the sealed windows look a long way off. Nor is it easy to move among the desks screwed to the floor because the desk lid is joined to the back of the seat in front. The person who usually sits behind Rubio every day, and is now behind her, is none other than Baragli.

Cándido López fought under the command of General Mitre. He did what soldiers always do in every war: tried to kill and avoid being killed. Like all the others, he did what he could to bear the rigours of the war with Paraguay, which were especially cruel. But he did not limit himself to the heroic or resigned efforts of a soldier obeying orders. He did more, he did something that was not asked or expected of him: showing a real talent and powers of observation, he made pencil sketches of scenes from the Argentinian army's campaign, including those of the disciplined chaos of open combat. News reached Mitre that a soldier in his ranks was making sketches that he hoped later to turn into great canvases depicting the war they were fighting. Mitre wanted to meet this curious soldier-painter. He received him, saw his sketches, asked his name, encouraged him to continue. Cándido López was very good at capturing the vast skies, the flattened earth, the wild, dank marshes, the scattered formations of the troops on the ground.

At the battle of Curupaití he lost a hand: the right hand, the one he used to paint with. An exploding grenade damaged it beyond repair. The wound did not heal as was hoped, and after a few days gangrene set in. As a result, his whole arm had to be amputated. This made it impossible for him to continue fighting, so that he was sent back to Buenos Aires. Although to history the War of the Triple Alliance was still going on, for him it was over. From that moment on he used his other hand. He was less good at first, until he acquired the skill needed to paint left-handed and do it well. He achieved this in the same way that everything is achieved: through hard work and determination. And so he embarked on his great work: a comprehensive demonstration of what war was.

Miss Perotti waves to María Teresa as a signal for her to start. The projector's mechanism is rudimentary. It seems as though it is getting stuck, but this is in fact how it functions. The first slide is very blurred. It needs to be focussed, by twisting the lens between two fingers. María Teresa does this until the image becomes clear. It is a painting of a flat plain dotted with tiny figures rendered with intricate brush-strokes. The soldiers, cannons, and rifles, the sheltering tents and the glow from the camp-fires: all look like miniatures. The next slide is better: it shows the sky, the huge sky. The space looks immense. A panoramic scene from an elevated viewpoint. Miss Perotti's pointer shows the intense green of the vegetation, the heavy trees, the slash of a river running between them. The men are painted red, with no faces. The brush-strokes bring them to life: López paints distance, but also treats each tiny detail with care. With the projector's clunky mechanism, María Teresa shows one image after another. The pointer hovers: notice the perfect combination of the precise and the diffuse. And now, war itself. The war, Curupaití. A similar high vantage point, a panorama, the battle. Cándido López is unaware of the cinema, because it does not yet exist, but to some extent he anticipates it. A scrawl: the smoke from the cannons, fading to white, mingling at the edges with the clouds in the blue sky. In his vision of the battle, López shows he is an expert in simultaneity. This is how a battle is: the overall view, with everyone engaged in combat, the way it might be seen by a general, a strategist, an artist, or God, and yet at the same time it is each individual soldier's combat, each one trying to save his skin: this one slashing with his sword, this one being slashed, one firing his rifle, another falling, another crouching down, another running away, another in his death agony, another already dead, this one too, and this one, this one as well. Everyone is fighting, and so is every individual: Cándido López paints them all and each and every one of them. The pointer comes to a halt, tapping the screen.

—Look here. Don't let your attention wander, look at this.

What is she pointing at? A fallen man. Fallen but not dead, only wounded, in the midst of the chaos of the battle of Curupaití. He is wounded: you can see the blood,

Cándido López's scarlet. He has been hit, struck down: he is not going to die, but he is wounded. Wounded in a part of his body that is not life-threatening, but which he will miss. It is his hand that is wounded. A tiny detail in the painting of the Battle of Curupaití. It is obvious what this is: Cándido López has painted himself. Tiny, almost invisible, but a self-portrait all the same. Perhaps the most discreet, the most indirect portrait possible; but there it is. An all-embracing view of war, and at one particular point in it, Candido López himself. He himself with his wound. Marré raises his hand, asking permission to speak. Miss Perotti gives it.

—What I like about this painter is that he was in the thick of the war, but he paints it as if he had not been there.

María Teresa is taken aback, or perhaps simply surprised, at Marré's observation. Not at what he has said, which she does not consider, but at the mere fact that he spoke at all. Miss Perotti had been talking so fluently and firmly it had not occurred to her that anyone could interrupt her flow. But Marré did just that. Miss Perotti listens to him approvingly, writes something down in the corresponding box in her marks book. Then she comments on what he said, with arguments that María Teresa does not entirely follow. Not that she completely ignores the progress of the lesson, even though she is the class assistant and not a pupil, and has to show the slides while making sure everyone is behaving themselves. She is interested in the topic and, besides, she likes the sound of Miss Perotti's voice. Yet occasionally her mind does wander; she thinks about things that have nothing to do with what is being explained, precisely because she is the assistant rather than a pupil. Sometimes also she is aware of something her eyes cannot see but which her mind is only too aware of, namely that Baragli is seated directly behind her. She has no reason to suppose he is not looking straight ahead of him at the screen, the slides, the work of Cándido López. She has no reason to suppose he might be looking at her, her shoulders or her hair, as she is so near to him. Yet that is what she does think, and this thought makes her lose concentration. She imagines she is, not at Baragli's mercy, which would be unthinkable, but at the mercy of his gaze. Perhaps he is putting his hand, apparently absentmindedly, on the surface of the desk. The wooden top is scratched, and in one corner there is a hole where the pupils once used to have ink-wells. Perhaps Baragli has put his hand in there, pretending not to notice, and is playing at moving his fingers even closer to her. María Teresa feels her neck stiffen at a possible contact, even though she knows this could never happen.

Cándido López has also painted a proper self-portrait. Not like the distant, coded portrait of him at the Battle of Curupaití, but a conventional, straightforward one, with his face in the foreground. It is somewhat odd, however, a strange depiction of his features. There is a look of fear on his reticent face. His hair also catches the attention, because it is stuck to his head bizarrely, as if he used brilliantine in the much later style of some tango singers. López's pose reveals anxiety, fear in the mouth and eyes, like someone who has been snapped unawares by a photographer, not a person posing for a portrait.

—That is because López is not posing for his portrait, he is painting himself. López is looking at himself reflected in a mirror. The face expresses the impression he has on seeing himself.

The bell rings at length, and the art lesson is over. Miss Perotti stuffs her things into her briefcase. María Teresa takes the carousel out of the projector, and removes the slides they have just seen one by one. She puts them away, also one by one, in the cardboard box where they are kept. The pupils meanwhile get up from their desks, ready to leave the room for their break. Baragli does so with the others, and as he heads for the door he passes very close to María Teresa. She is sitting down putting away the slides as he walks through the narrow gap between the two rows of desks. The edge of his blue blazer brushes against her hand. This contact brings her fingers to a halt, as if someone had suddenly called her name. María Teresa forces herself to resume her task, but cannot avoid sniffing at the scent Baragli gives off as he goes by. Possibly she is hoping to confirm the familiar smell of black tobacco, the one she remembers from her father after dinner in her childhood. But she discovers something different, which surprises her without really disappointing her. Baragli has a strong scent of men's cologne. Although it is not too outlandish to wear cologne to school, she was not expecting it, or at least not from Baragli.

The scent penetrates her nostrils and stays with her. Later on she brings it back, almost at will, so that it is not clear if she is actually recalling it or if it is still in her head. Before the day is over (her work day, the school day) Señor Biasutto comes up to her and confirms they are to meet the following Monday. It is better if they see each other in an out-of-the-way bar, where they are unlikely to run into any pupils from the school. The students like to fantasize and immediately invent things. They agree to meet on Monday at half-past seven in the evening in a dimly-lit bar on the corner of Balcarce and Moreno, well away from anywhere the pupils usually frequent.

As she leaves, María Teresa feels happy. It is early June and the weather is cold, more so than in other years. In spite of this, she is happy, although it is already dark when she leaves the school, and this has not been a good day as far as her investigations in the boys' toilet are concerned. Quite simply, she is happy. She does not head straight for home as she usually does. First she has to go to a pharmacy to buy a new box of anti-depressants for the mother. She has only a few left, and has asked María Teresa to do her this favour. She is clutching one of the prescriptions that a cousin gets for them in exchange for other favours in the hospital where he works. She also has the card that entitles them to a fifteen per cent discount. It shows a twenty-year-old photograph of her mother looking as she did when María Teresa was born.

On the corner of Alsina and Defensa there is a pharmacy that María Teresa particularly likes, because its windows, lettering, and the counter, even the coloured bottles lined up on the shelves, lend it the old-fashioned look of the old Buenos Aires chemist shops. She likes all the glass and the stylish decorative writing. She has come to buy her mother's medication, but almost as soon as she enters she sees something she had never noticed before: the fact that this pharmacy, like many others in the city, has a section devoted to perfumes. Timidly, she goes over to have a look at this part of the shop. She sees the rows of deodorant, the pots of skin cream, nail varnishes, the unsteady piles of toilet soaps. None of this attracts her attention, but when she reaches the shelf containing the boxes and bottles of men's cologne she comes to a halt. There are lots of them, none of which she knows. She invents a family birthday for the female assistant, and asks if it is allowed to try them.

—You can smell them, but not try them on.

First of all, María Teresa chooses a red box with a blue sailing ship on it: she sniffs it and puts it back. She tries another called Crandall. It comes in a long-necked bottle, with an unusual label hanging from it. She likes it, but that is not the one. The next one she tries is called Ginell: its box shows a pair of polo ponies. Not that one either. She tries again with a more recent brand called Colbert. It is in a dark green box, perhaps British racing green, but she cannot be sure. As soon as she brings it up to her nostrils, she realises it is the cologne Baragli was wearing. Now she knows that Baragli uses this cologne, that he must have a box the same as this one in his bathroom at home. She decides to buy it, and hands the box to the assistant, who has been hovering somewhat suspiciously around her. María Teresa is not sure why she is buying it and taking it with her.

—Is it a gift?

—Yes.

There are no men in her house. Her father has left, and her brother is in the south of the country. The truth is that María Teresa is not thinking of them: neither her brother who sends postcards, nor her father who does not even do that. She does not think of them, or Baragli; at most, although it might be going too far to call it thinking, she is beguiled by the scent of Colbert cologne as she watches the assistant skilfully wrap the box in gift wrapping and stick it down until she has made a perfect package, then as a finishing touch add a silver sticker that says 'Happy Birthday!'

María Teresa has been so busy she almost forgets to buy what she came for: her mother's anti-depressants. She remembers just in time because when she takes out her purse to pay for the cologne, the benefits card falls out, and the black-and-white face of her youthful mother lies open on the counter.

—Oh, I almost forgot.

A short while later she is travelling on her own in the metro, a small plastic bag in one hand. Inside it, there are two boxes: one wrapped, the other not. The fragrance of the cologne is so strong it fills the bag, penetrating beyond the bottle, the box, its wrapping. Every so often María Teresa peeps inside, as if she were keeping a small pet (a tortoise, a hamster, or a newly-born kitten) there, and has to check periodically to see it is all right and has not suffocated. She decides that as soon as she gets home, even before she gives her mother her new box of pills to put in the bathroom cabinet, she will put the Colbert cologne away in her bedside table drawer.

She goes in, to find a new postcard from her brother on the dining-room table. It was sent from Bahía Blanca. All it says is: Francisco. This time the mother, who these days only occasionally cries, has read it, and says she does not understand why her son wrote nothing more than his name. María Teresa explains with a vague reflection on the lack of time and the cost of words (the mother knows it is a postcard and not a telegram, but says nothing in reply). However, the photograph on the other side does not show Bahía Blanca, as if the city lacked any places of interest that would justify making a postcard of them. Or perhaps there were some, but Francisco did not choose one. The fact is that, despite posting it in Bahía Blanca, the postcard he has sent shows a nearby resort called Monte Hermoso. The locals are proud of the fact that this is the only place in Argentina where the sun both rises and sets over the ocean in the same bay. The photographs on the card show this, because it is divided in two: in one half the word 'sunrise' is written, over a view of deserted sand and sea, with the sun peeping over the horizon, while in the other half is written the word 'sunset', over a golden beach where two women, in noticeably old-fashioned bathing costumes, are watching the sun go down with dreamy expressions on their faces. Although these two juxtaposed photographs depict inconsequential scenes of summer and holidays, they also remind mother and daughter of what they had already realised: that Francisco now really is by the sea. Not that far away, it is true, and still within the boundaries of the province of Buenos Aires, but on the coast now rather than in the heart of the pampas. Further south and on the coast, truly on the edge of the Atlantic.

—We never went to Monte Hermoso. Your cousins used to go occasionally, years ago.

—My cousins?

—Yes.

—And did they like it?

—They said they did, but they complained a lot. They said the sea was full of jelly fish that stung them.

Shortly afterwards, the panorama darkens still further. They might still receive a postcard of Monte Hermoso, stamped in Bahía Blanca. But that would simply be a confirmation of the delays in the postal service, because Francisco will no longer be there: he is being transferred. With a single phone token that allows only a brief burst of words, he calls to tell them he is going to be put on a plane and taken even further south. Further: to Comodoro Rivadavia. No, no, that's not in Buenos Aires province any more, it's in Chubut. Yes, yes, Patagonia. No, no, no, not in trucks, in an Air Force plane called a Hercules. Hercules, yes: Hercules. No, no, no, he doesn't know anything; nobody knows anything. Yes, yes, on the coast: right beside the sea.

10

María Teresa is busy filling in forms in the assistants' room when she suddenly feels the urge to go to the toilet. She no longer even thinks of doing what might be expected of her: going to the women's toilet reserved for the assistants. Neither there nor the toilet for girl pupils: instead, she heads straight for the boys' toilet. As always, she enters without being seen or making any noise, and almost without thinking chooses the first cubicle. She really needs to wee, and so raises her skirt and takes off her knickers. She settles over the hole in order to use it as quickly as possible, but even so it takes time for her to relax and for the liquid to start to flow. While she is crouched there, she hears the swing doors go and realises a pupil is coming into the toilet. She holds back, and listens intently in order not to disturb the solitude the pupil must take for granted as he goes over to the urinal, unzips his trousers and prepares to urinate. Possibly he also needs the pause of some kind of prelude, because it is clear that everything is ready for him to perform, and yet nothing happens. Perhaps the cold in the toilet inhibits him as it does María Teresa. She also feels strange, because she is there with her skirt pulled up and nothing underneath. The air inside the toilet is so cold it is almost like being out in the quad. The body has to get used to it, because it is difficult to do anything if its organs are clenched tight. The pupil eventually succeeds, perhaps by fondling his thing a little to warm it. María Teresa is aware of the exact moment he starts urinating, because by now she knows the sound it produces so well. Yet instead of withdrawing into complete anonymity in the presence of a urinating pupil (a satisfied but discreet sentinel), in this instance, to her surprise she also starts to wee. She does so as quietly as possible, even though she is still running a risk. She does it on impulse, a sudden whim, although she has to admit to herself that the desire has been growing within her for several days. She urinates at the same time as the pupil: close by him, and with him. Not in the same way, of course, because he is a boy; not in the same way but in the same place, and better still, at the same time. Only a thin partition separates them, and that only partially keeps them apart, while at the same time making their actions doubly simultaneous. The two sounds merge into one (that is why she is not heard), and so do their actions.

If, as she rarely does, she were ever to think about all this, María Teresa would perhaps at most admit to a vague, wavering sense of personal satisfaction, attributed above all to the audacity she is showing in carrying out her duties. People do not always fail to do their duty out of moral laziness, but sometimes out of sheer cowardice. She, on the other hand, is showing great courage in this game of espionage that she has taken on as part of her job. She looks forward to the moment when Señor Biasutto congratulates her for enabling the drastic punishment of all those boys who secretly smoke in the school toilets. And just like spies in films, she has had to venture into hostile territory, which is always a risky business. The authorities will praise her for her daring while they are deciding the sanctions such a flagrant breach of regulations demands.

The boy finishes urinating, and María Teresa stops at the same time. She has no idea whether this was simply another coincidence, bound to happen following the initial one, or if she in some way forced herself to finish with him so that the pleasing simultaneity would not come to an end. With sufficient will-power it is possible to dominate one's bodily needs, and if necessary interrupt them. María Teresa finishes, or interrupts herself (the difference is unimportant), and stops weeing in the cubicle at the exact moment the pupil finishes at the urinal. He must now be shaking his thing, in an unfathomable rite of drips and endings. As everyone knows, women have to be more thorough about the cleaning process. They need paper and have to dry themselves. María Teresa does this now, her hand blindly bringing a sheet of pink, absorbent paper up to her lower body. She holds it there without rubbing; although she does move it slightly. Just the other side of the partition, the pupil shakes himself, looks down and sees himself; María Teresa rests her hand against her body a little longer than necessary to dry herself. She experiences the tingling sensation again, which she takes to mean she wants to wee. She might wonder why she is getting this sensation at that very moment, when she only finished weeing a second ago, and be surprised. But instead she thinks it must be because she controlled herself before she had properly finished.

The pupil is meticulous; he washes his hands with soap before leaving the toilet. While he is putting his hands under the cold water tap, or rubbing them vigorously on the elongated sphere of the soap, he hums a song. He hums or murmurs a melody, rather than singing it out loud; it is impossible to make out the words and, although the tune sounds familiar, María Teresa cannot put a name to it. Even so, the boy's voice is quite clear: his pronunciation is indistinct, and the notes waver, but of itself his activity is clear, and this means María Teresa is able to recognise and therefore identify it, or more accurately to identify the pupil it belongs to. It sounds so familiar to her that she is certain it must be one of the pupils from third year class ten. She thinks, remembers, tries to associate it. There are two boys who have similar voices: Babenco and Valenzuela. She thinks back to when they call out 'Present' as she does the register. She recalls their voices and confirms to herself that, yes, it was one or other of them she just heard in the toilet: it was Babenco or Valenzuela who had been there, who had urinated close to her while she was doing the same thing.

Shortly afterwards she is sitting in the classroom, performing her assistant's role (but no, she is wrong, she is underestimating herself; when she is in the toilet, in the cubicle, she is also fulfilling her role). The first break has finished, and third year class ten have a Spanish lesson. All the pupils have lined up, stood apart, gone into their classrooms, and have sat down. Now they have to wait, in perfect silence of course, for their respective teachers to arrive. The teachers take four or five minutes to finish their break-time coffee, leave the carpeted room they have on the ground floor, climb the stairs, walk along the cloisters, and reach the doors to the classrooms. While they are doing this, the assistants stand in front of each class to make sure the pupils are well-behaved. María Teresa casts her watchful eye over them all. At some point, however, this typical gaze of a vigilant assistant ceases – not to be watchful, but to be directed at all of them. Instead, it is aimed at Valenzuela, at Babenco. Her scanning lingers longer than necessary when it picks up their two faces. Babenco and Valenzuela: one of them (she does not know which) sang in the boys' toilet before the break. Their voices are similar, throaty but still child-like, and it is as easy to distinguish them from the other boys as it is to confuse them with each other. One or other of them asked Miss Pesotto, who took the Physics lesson that morning, for permission to go to the toilet, and went there to urinate. Something strange now happens to María Teresa. A lot of what went on during the few moments she was in the boys' toilet was based on a single premise: that the pupil who was so close to her was completely unaware that the class assistant, in other words her, was urinating at the same time. And yet now, back in the classroom, while she is ensuring the pupils are quiet before Mr Ilundain comes in, she seeks out the eyes of Babenco and Valenzuela as if they could not possibly be unaware of what had happened a short while earlier, as if something (an intuition or instinct) must reveal to them what took place in the toilet, and that it would take only a chance meeting of their gazes for that complicity to be restored and for them to recognise each other. To some extent, María Teresa cannot believe she can have been alongside Babenco or Valenzuela, that she can have been drying herself without looking while they, or one of them, Babenco or Valenzuela (she does not know which), was looking down while he shook his thing, and that now there should remain no trace of such closely-shared intimacy in their eyes, no immediate flash of recognition when their gazes meet. There ought at least to be some kind of recollection, an echo of what they experienced together; she tries to revive this by giving them an intent, knowing look. However, all she finds in Babenco's eyes is the blank look typical of the dolt (Babenco is a hopeless student, constantly failing his subjects), while Valenzuela looks absentminded, obviously somewhere else. (Valenzuela is good at chess: he is training himself in the art of concentrating on one thing to the exclusion of everything else.)

María Teresa will not give up: she stares at them as though to force them to admit a truth she imagines they are denying. It is as though this were a session of hypnosis, but performed backwards: snapping the fingers to put the person into a trance, and staring at them fixedly to wake them up. This waking up would lead to an awareness, if no more than a dim and half-disclosed one, of what had happened between her and one of them in the boys' toilet. It does not occur to her to speculate that the lack of response from their evasive eyes might be a clear sign that Babenco or Valenzuela, whichever one it was, are well aware of what took place, that they know it somehow, because the body registers certain things on its own behalf and only later, by some obscure means or other, reveals them. It does not occur to María Teresa (or she prefers not to) to think in this way: what she wants is to catch their eyes (Babenco's or Valenzuela's) and, by doing so, provoke a flash of intoxicating recognition.

She does not succeed, and her attempt is put to an end by the arrival of Mr Ilundain.

—On your feet, if you please.

The absolute rule that the school pupils receive their teachers standing by their desks is observed yet again. They will not sit down until Mr Ilundain has greeted them and told them they may do so. María Teresa leaves the course book open on the teacher's desk, asks permission to leave, and steps down from the platform with short, energetic strides. As she leaves the classroom she closes the door behind her. No sooner is she outside than she collapses against the wall. She stares at the dim light that is a permanent feature of the quad. She feels dizzy. Her hands are troubled by a slight tremor; her back is prickly with sudden perspiration. It is not that she feels hot: she is only wearing a flowery blouse and over it an old cardigan with big buttons her mother knitted for her years ago, nothing that would stifle her. Marcelo, the assistant for third year class eight, comes out of his room because the Latin teacher has arrived, and passes by her.

—Everything all right?

—Yes, fine.

That same afternoon, or that same evening, she meets Señor Biasutto. The bar they have agreed on is sufficiently far from the school to allay the head of the assistants' fears that they might be seen by pupils, but not so far away as to imply the two of them are out of the work sphere. It is as if they tacitly concur that this is a simple extension of the kind of conversation they usually have in the assistants' room at school or in the quad during break-time. It is not the same, for example, as meeting on a Saturday afternoon or having dinner together.

Señor Biasutto arrives after María Teresa, but does not

keep her waiting long. He was held up at school by a last-minute problem. Nothing serious, just an organizational matter he had to see the Deputy Headmaster about. Señor Biasutto looks relaxed and in a good mood. María Teresa notices that if he smiles broadly, his moustache stretches so far it almost disappears.

—I suggested we came here as a precaution, if that's all right. The pupils are at an age when they fantasize a lot, and there's no reason we should encourage them.

The waiter comes over to their table. María Teresa asks for a milky coffee, with more milk than coffee; Señor Biasutto orders a shot of Old Smuggler whisky without ice. He sits leaning forward, both elbows on the table. María Teresa has never studied him at such close quarters before. He uses brilliantine on his black hair, and the skin on his face is blotchy. His shirt collar is starched, and the knot on his tie is larger than normal. He hardly ever blinks: his eyes are like black holes. His teeth are hidden behind his inexpressive mouth.

—Tell me about you, María Teresa.

—About me?

—Yes, you.

María Teresa blushes. She says she does not know what to say.

—Tell me about your life. Who do you live with?

Slightly hesitant, María Teresa tells him she lives with her mother in a small apartment in Palermo. With her mother and brother, but for the moment she is not counting her brother because he has been called up. As a girl she lived a lot further out, in Villa del Parque.

Señor Biasutto drops a gold packet of dark tobacco

cigarettes onto the table.

—What about your father?

— My father?

—Yes, your father.

María Teresa swallows.

—My father died.

—My goodness! I'm sorry to hear that.

—It was a long time ago.

—I'm really sorry.

To change the subject and so as not to appear too dull, María Teresa tells him she is thinking of continuing her studies, although for the moment she has not chosen what subject, and is not sure what she would like to do.

—Women have a good choice of careers these days.

Señor Biasutto lights a cigarette with a silver-plated lighter that he quickly slips back into his jacket pocket. He blows the smoke out of his nostrils, obscuring his moustache, and his eyes wrinkle. He smiles again as he does this.

—Thanks to my mother I'm good at knitting. She knitted this cardigan I'm wearing.

Señor Biasutto raises an eyebrow: the right one.

—It's a beautiful cardigan. And it looks very good on you.

This time María Teresa blushes so much she has to lower her head to her chest.

—Señor Biasutto!

Señor Biasutto advances a hand across the table, appears to change his mind, and leaves it inconclusively by the pile of napkins and the ashtray where his cigarette is dangling.

—María Teresa, please, don't be so formal! Did you call

me Señor Biasutto? We're not at work now. Here you must call me Carlos.

—Carlos. What a nice name.

The waiter brings their orders: a milky coffee for María Teresa, a whisky with no ice for Señor Biasutto. María Teresa tears open two sachets of sugar and pours them into her cup. The sound is like sand falling through an hourglass, but dies away as soon as the sugar hits the pale liquid.

—You put two in, do you?

—Sugar, you mean?

—Yes, sugar.

—Yes, I put two in.

—Quite right. There's enough bitterness in life already, isn't there?

Señor Biasutto smiles to himself, and so does María Teresa when he hastily explains it was just his little joke. The philosophy he lives by, he explains, is in no way pessimistic. After this there is a silence they both fill with another exchange of smiles. These soon fade, however, and so María Teresa decides to add that she also thinks of herself as a cheerful person. Then they both fall silent again: Señor Biasutto smokes his cigarette, and María Teresa stirs the sugar in her cup.

—Some sugar sachets have sayings on them, wise sayings.

At this, Señor Biasutto, who had been leaning back in his chair, now bends forward again, resting his head on his hands.

—Do you like wise sayings?

María Teresa nods.

—Yes, I do. They teach us how to live.

—That's true. I find there are some sayings that leave me

131

thinking. Human beings are such complex creatures. The problem is I have a poor memory, I read things I think are going to be engraved on my mind forever, but when I try to repeat them they've gone out of my mind.

—I don't have much of a memory either. That's why I have a little book I call my 'notebook for wise sayings'. Whenever I come across a memorable saying, I write it down.

—I like to hear you talking about these things, María Teresa.

María Teresa feels her cheeks flushing again. This time though she is not ashamed. Perhaps Señor Biasutto appreciates her shyness.

—Do you remember one?

—One what?

—One of the phrases you've jotted down in your book of wise sayings.

—I'll have to think.

—We're in no hurry, are we?

Señor Biasutto smiles a fixed smile, as if waiting for someone to take his photograph. María Teresa meanwhile is thinking.

—Oh yes, I've got one.

—Let's hear it.

—It goes like this: 'If you shed tears because the sun has set, you will not see the stars shining.'

—What a lovely phrase!

—It's very wise, isn't it?

—Yes, and very profound.

—I often say it to my mother, when I can see she is depressed.

—Is your mother a sad person then?

—She's worried about my brother.

—That's logical, isn't it? But things will be all right. You have to keep faith.

—Yes.

Still staring at her, Señor Biasutto drinks from his glass. His eyebrows are so bushy they almost join in the middle. María Teresa takes advantage of leaning forward to take a long sip of her coffee in order to hide her face and try to control her nerves.

—And what other plans do you have for your life?

María Teresa was not paying attention, and so the question takes her by surprise.

—What did you say?

—I was simply curious to know what other plans you have for your life.

María Teresa blinks and says nothing. Señor Biasutto uses her confusion to stretch his hand out again. He is wearing a large ring with the initials CB on it. He rests his hand on the napkin-holder in the middle of the table.

—I mean, María Teresa, such a pretty girl like you.

María Teresa's face immediately turns a bright red, as if someone has flicked an electric switch. She feels hot.

—Oh, Señor Biasutto, don't say such things.

—Of course I'll say them, María Teresa. Such a pretty, well-educated and sensitive young woman like you. Have you ever thought of getting married?

If she could bury her head in her hands and reply without being seen, as she does in the confessional, María Teresa would do so now.

—Not yet. There's time enough.

Señor Biasutto taps his stubby fingers on the sheaf of napkins.

—Yes, I can imagine: you're still very young. But perhaps there's a candidate at least?

Swallowing hard and finding it difficult to speak, María Teresa merely wags a finger in denial. Shaking her head, she lowers her gaze, and although she cannot directly see him, she knows Señor Biasutto is smiling again. She sees his hand draw back towards the cigarette still burning in the ashtray. He raises it to his sour mouth. Ash falls from the tip, a light, greyish ash. Part of it falls onto the table, part onto Señor Biasutto's clothes.

María Teresa finishes her coffee and stares at the grounds in the bottom of her cup.

Outside, the street grows quiet.

11

No, she would rather not have another cup of coffee. Not that she is worried about insomnia, which she suffers from anyway, but because too much coffee could produce stomach acidity. Señor Biasutto, though, orders another whisky, again with no ice. He insists María Teresa has something: she cannot leave him drinking on his own. She suddenly realises her mouth is dry, with a sticky taste; she feels thirsty. A soft drink perhaps? She asks for a Tab. While the waiter is removing their things and bringing their new order, they barely speak. However discreet he may be, the waiter is an intruder, and they have to wait for him to finish. When he finally moves off, leaving the soft drinks bottle and the whisky glass on the table, it is María Teresa rather than Señor Biasutto who renews the conversation.

—Your job at school must be hard, mustn't it?

Taken by surprise, Señor Biasutto does not reply.

—I mean, being in charge of all those assistants. So much responsibility! That must make things hard, doesn't it?

Señor Biasutto presses his back against the chair, as if someone were trying to get past behind him and he had to prevent them doing so.

— It's a job with a lot of responsibility.

— I'm new at the school, but even I can see that.

— You're very efficient and pay close attention.

— How long have you worked at the school?

— I took up the post in nineteen-seventy-five.

— Seventy-five? Seven years ago!

— Yes.

— When did you become supervisor of the assistants?

— So many questions, María Teresa. You're like a journalist. Or a detective.

— It's just that I'm curious.

— From the start, my post was as head of the assistants.

It is only now that María Teresa realises Señor Biasutto is rather put out. She reproaches herself for not having seen this earlier. She falls silent, wishing she had not asked anything. Señor Biasutto does not speak either. A bus goes along the street: they both pay close attention to it, as though they were watching a film in a cinema and did not want to miss anything. It is a Number 29; its indicator board says it is going from La Boca out to Olivos. María Teresa fills her glass, and the black liquid fizzes. If Señor Biasutto's whisky had any ice in it, he could stir it with a finger now, just to keep his hands busy. Since it does not have any, he takes out a second cigarette and lights it. The one he has already finished lies crumpled in the ashtray, its final shape a useless butt. When he breathes out the first mouthful of the fresh smoke, Señor Biasutto feels soothed: it has the same effect as a long sigh. María Teresa, on the other hand, is still embarrassed. An empty sachet is lying on the table: she picks it up and with manic precision starts tearing it into tiny pieces, as though it were a secret letter which, once it had been read, had to be removed from the face of the earth.

By now, Señor Biasutto feels ready to resume his former smiling state, and so decides to rescue María Teresa from her dejection.

—Don't get me wrong, I like it when you ask me questions.

María Teresa raises her eyes, and he smiles at her.

—I like you asking me them.

María Teresa smiles back at him, although her cheeks are still scarlet.

Señor Biasutto explains.

—The thing is, when I began it was a very complicated time for our country. The fabric of our society was under threat, se we had to act with absolute determination.

It is María Teresa's turn to let her hands wander over the table-top.

—They say at school that you were outstanding in that respect.

Señor Biasutto smiles, shrugging modestly.

—I only did what anyone in my position would have done.

María Teresa insists.

—But you were the one who did it. The others might possibly have done the same, but it was you who did it.

Señor Biasutto waves his hands either to dispel the smoke or María Teresa's words. He wants to avoid any hint of adulation, or at least to get back to the previous topic of conversation. When he drops his hands again, he lays them on the table, inevitably close to María Teresa's. Seeing this, she is paralysed, unable to move hers. She knows they are talking about the famous lists, and, unconcerned at his obvious reluctance to say much about the subject, feels she has been let into his confidence in an extraordinary way. Perhaps this is why she allows Señor Biasutto to do what he does next: to slowly touch her fingers.

—I can't see any engagement ring.

As he says this, his face twists into another smile.

—No, I'm not engaged.

Señor Biasutto lowers his head. Some strands of brilliantined hair refuse to move with the rest, and stay sticking straight up.

—A pretty girl like you.

María Teresa withdraws her hand, but not hurriedly.

—Time enough for that.

He nods, thoughtfully.

—Yes, there's a time for everything, isn't there?

—That's what my father always used to say: there's no point rushing things in life.

Another silence falls between them; the street too is silent.

—I'm really sorry about your father.

—Thank you.

In the early evening, the customers in these central bars all look as if they were pressed from the same mould: office workers tired after a hard day's work who even so cannot face the idea of returning home; pairs of people who come to tell each other what they had no chance to talk about during the day. As the evening advances, however, the clientele changes. Whereas a lot of people come to work in this part of the city, almost no-one lives here. While there is still light in the sky, wild-eyed, gloomy-looking individuals emerge from hidden corners and come into the bars to sit idly in front of a drink, waiting for a supper that will probably never arrive.

Absorbed in their conversation, at first neither María Teresa nor Señor Biasutto notices this change. They are talking about different periods in the life of Argentina: the good old days when there was respect and one's word was one's bond, the hippie era when filth and promiscuity threatened to take over the world, the years of terrorism and bombs planted in kindergartens. Señor Biasutto has lived much longer than María Teresa and therefore knows more about these things. The kids of today are better behaved and more docile, but that does not mean they are not at the mercy of foreign ideas or the dangers their whirling hormones lead them into. The dangers of the past were greater, and therefore all the more evident. The ones young people face now work surreptitiously and demand a stricter, more constant vigilance.

—Read history, María Teresa: that will teach you. Each time a war is won, what follows is the tracking down of the last remnants of the losing side. Snipers, lost stragglers, the desperate. It is more like a cleansing operation than a battle, but don't be deceived, it is still war!

María Teresa listens to his words with the fervour of a disciple, although she knows she does not completely understand everything Señor Biasutto is saying. Despite appearing to be entirely caught up in his explanation, she suddenly notices that the atmosphere in the café has changed around her. She realises it is growing late even before she glances down at the loose-fitting lady's watch on her wrist. By now she is the only woman there. Apart from her, there is Señor Biasutto sitting opposite, the manager counting change at the till, the two waiters who by now have little to do, an elderly man staring at the crust left over from a sandwich that no longer exists, an Alistair Maclean reader who does not care that his coffee is growing cold, a tea-drinker with a highly-developed sense of how it should be prepared, two *grappa* drinkers leaning on the bar.

—It's getting a bit late for me, Señor Biasutto.

—It may be late for you, but you're still calling me Señor Biasutto.

—Carlos?

—Carlos.

—It's rather late for me, Carlos. And I have to confess something.

—A confession? Tell me.

—In my family they don't call me María Teresa.

—Ah, no?

—No.

—What do they call you?

—They call me . . . they call me Marita.

—Marita?

—Yes.

—But that's lovely!

—It is?

—Of course it is. And put away your purse, Marita, this instant. I insist on paying. And let me accompany you home.

Knowing she is blushing again, María Teresa plucks up her courage.

—I'll agree to let you pay. But let's leave the other for another time.

— No point rushing things, eh?

María Teresa smiles.

—Yes, that's right.

They say goodbye at the street corner. The cold outside probably cuts the farewells and polite exchanges to a minimum. Señor Biasutto appears to be trying to find something to say, but in vain. He seems preoccupied, as though he were about to miss a train but cannot make his mind up to run for it, afraid he might not only lose the train but also his composure. Eventually he bends towards María Teresa in a sort of bow. He takes her hand, clutching her fingers in his. He kisses them, and she can feel his prickly moustache across her knuckles.

—See you tomorrow, Marita.

María Teresa returns home in a confused state of mind. She is pleased with herself for having dared to meet a man like Señor Biasutto. A real man, as her mother would call him. A knowledgeable, experienced man, courageous, a gentleman, well-educated. At the same time though she is mortified to think he must have found her very dull. Perhaps she should have told him about how she studied the piano when she was little, or tell him more of the 'wise sayings' she has noted down in her book, which seemed to interest him. And perhaps she should not have allowed herself to blush so often, although this was not something she could control, still less pester him with questions about his job, which obviously upset him. It troubles her to think that after this first experience Señor Biasutto will not want to get to know her more. A man like him, who provided such vital services in the most difficult moments of Argentina's history, such a thoughtful, profound man, must have found her insipid. This is what she always feels, and this evening was no exception. An extraordinary man with a drab, unimpressive girl.

It is also true, however, that he offered to accompany her home, and that she was the one who refused. Perhaps he was only being polite, because night had fallen and she is a woman. Yet when they parted he kissed her hand, like princes do, in an obvious act of gallantry. He brushed his lips against the back of her hand, even if it was not his mouth she felt, but the prickliness of his moustache. The moustache reminds her of a football player she thinks is called Angel Labruna, or possibly a tango singer, most likely Goyeneche (two men she had heard of as a girl through her father, who was a River Plate fan and followed Aníbal Troilo's tango orchestra).

Will she get another chance to talk to Señor Biasutto alone and without the pressure of time? She would like to think so. Today she learnt he is called Carlos, like Carlos Gardel, a very manly name. In return for this, she has told him her secret: that at home she is known as Marita. As far as she can tell, this revelation pleased him; in fact, from then on that was what he began to call her (whilst she, on the other hand, out of nervousness or embarrassment, made the mistake of continuing to call him Señor Biasutto, even after he had asked her not to). It would be odd for him to be so familiar as to call her Marita, and to allow her to call him Carlos, and then not to want to meet again as they had done that evening. Odd, but not impossible, if Señor Biasutto found her boring, or had thought she was more worthwhile than she in fact turned out to be.

She arrives home late and thinks she ought to give her mother some explanation. She will tell her the truth: that she met a man in a café near the school. But she will immediately add what kind of man he is: an exceptional

man. And in addition, her boss. She will not tell her
about the lists, because the mother might not be able to
appreciate that, but will say that at school he is regarded
as a hero wreathed in modesty (like José de San Martín).
She foresees in great detail how the conversation with her
mother will go. She imagines her being interested and
even approving, although doubtless she will give her lots
of advice and warnings to take care. But when she arrives
at the flat, things do not go as anticipated. Francisco has
just phoned from Comodoro Rivadavia. How could she be
so late that she was not there when he called? The mother
talked to him. She is still too emotional to be able to
remember, or to repeat, exactly what they said. Francisco
explained, almost as if he were showing her a map, exactly
where he was now. He is a long way south. Further south
than Bahía Blanca, which is where he was before and which
is still part of Buenos Aires province. Further south than
Viedma, which is the southernmost limit of the province.
Even further south than Trelew, a name the mother recalls
because it was there years earlier that a group of terrorists
tried to escape, although almost all of them were soon
caught again. In the far south. And by the sea. Right on the
sea. And that is what Francisco said he did all the blessed
day: stare at the sea, stare at the sea, stare at the sea.

The mother started to tell him about her counting
aircraft, but at that moment, without any sort of warning,
the line went dead. All at once, while they were in mid-
conversation, the line suddenly gave the busy tone. They
did not even manage to say goodbye. The two of them,
mother and son, were unable to say goodbye to each other.
She sat waiting beside the telephone for a long while,

staring at the little picture of the Argentinian flag in the middle of the dial, thinking Francisco would call again at least to say goodbye. But he did not call back. More than an hour had gone by, and he had not called back.

María Teresa persuades her mother it cannot be easy to find telephone tokens down there, that the time allowed for them to speak to their families will be strictly controlled, and that there must be a really long line of Francisco's colleagues waiting to use the public telephone. Although she can see that this calms the mother down a lot, that she goes back to watching the TV news and is no longer crying, she stays with her in the kitchen and helps prepare their supper.

After they have eaten, María Teresa says she does not want any coffee, and yet despite this, when soon afterwards she goes to bed, she cannot sleep. She tosses and turns, her eyes wide open. She is thinking. She would like not to think so that she can finally get to sleep, but sleep does not come, and therefore she thinks. She thinks about Señor Biasutto. About the moment when he took hold of her fingers, the gallant kiss he gave her. She wonders yet again if there will be another such meeting between them. She knows, because it is common knowledge, that if there is it will be up to him to take the initiative, because he is the man and she is the woman. Despite this, she also considers what she could do to encourage this second meeting. Without behaving in a way that was unbecoming of a well-brought-up young woman, she could strike up some kind of conversation that returned or alluded to the one they had in the bar. Or when they greeted each other again at work she could call him Señor Biasutto, but with a glint in her eye which would remind him that on another occasion, at another moment, she had not called him that, but Carlos.

She is not sure she has it in her to behave like this: she thinks not. Other girls might find it easier, or even perfectly natural, to make insinuations or purposefully have a glint in their eye. It is quite possible, however, that she will be unable to pass by Señor Biasutto without immediately blushing and looking down at the floor. She is convinced he must have found her uninspiring. She hears the mother switch off the television in the dining-room and go to bed. It is late. Still she cannot get to sleep. She wonders whether a man who finds a woman uninspiring would give her the kind of kiss on the hand that Señor Biasutto gave her on the street corner opposite the church as they were saying farewell.

Suddenly, completely by chance, as if it were a sudden discovery made in a dream, María Teresa finds the way. That is what she calls it in her mind: the way. The way that will lead her to a second meeting with Señor Biasutto. If she catches the boys who hide in the toilet to smoke, that will give her an obvious reason for the two of them to have another conversation. And it is also obvious that conversation will be nothing like any of those they could have had before – say a week or ten days earlier – when he had not yet called her Marita and she had never called him Carlos. She will redouble her efforts to finally discover who the culprits are. This solution acts like an analgesic, and at last she falls asleep. The moment she wakes up the next morning, however, it is the first thought that comes into her head: that she has to redouble her efforts to uncover the pupils who are secretly smoking in the school toilet. Baragli or whoever else, pupils in her own class or in any others. That does not matter. What matters is to uncover them, denounce them, unleash the severe punishment that will act as a lesson to everyone else, and then receive the heartfelt congratulations of Señor Biasutto. Except that Señor Biasutto, who will congratulate her officially within the school, has already kissed her hand and called her Marita, and she has let him press his mouth (or at least his moustache) to her fingers, and has called him Carlos. So nothing can be the same as before.

The next day, the first two lessons are taken up with a concert organised by the school authorities with the title (which is also a slogan) of 'For Peace'. It is an organ concert under the direction of maestro De Zorzi. Together with its many other sources of pride, the school can boast the only pipe organ outside a church in the entire city of Buenos Aires. It is situated in the school's Great Hall, a place of subdued splendour where, to give but one example, Albert Einstein in person once gave a lecture on the Theory of Relativity. The Great Hall demands even stricter vigilance than normal: it is much larger than the classrooms, the pupils are more rowdy, and the rule that a boy should never sit next to a girl may sometimes not be completely followed (look at Baragli, for example, and how he has managed to seat himself right next to Dreiman).

Maestro De Zorzi has chosen a programme devoted entirely to baroque music. Bach is predominant, leavened with abundant doses of Vivaldi. The pupils seem to be following the music with relative interest. At least they are not openly inattentive, and during the concert there is little to admonish them over (Babenco twists on his chair at one point, Servelli squirms as if he were trying to stop laughing, Daciuk plays with the ribbons on her blouse: that is about all). Perhaps it is the fugue structure of much of the music which keeps their attention. Whenever there is a silence, the pupils all get ready to applaud, first checking the reaction of Mr Roel, in order to save themselves the embarrassment of applauding in the pause between movements in the belief that the work has come to an end.

The concert comes to a close and the pupils return to their classrooms. The music does not appear to have calmed them, as it is said to do with savage beasts, but on the contrary seems to have excited them. This may be due to the liveliness of the baroque compositions, or the satisfaction the pupils feel at going into the Great Hall, reserved for the grandest of school occasions (the aisles are carpeted, the chairs are velvet, there are balconies round the top, and splendid ceilings).

With the return to their classrooms, the routine of lessons resumes. So as not to waste any more time, as soon as Miss Urricarriet has arrived and she no longer has to supervise third year form ten, María Teresa hastens to the area of the boys' toilet. Still taking all necessary precautions to avoid being seen, she enters the toilet as quickly as possible. Once inside, she feels contented. She chooses a cubicle; not the first, which is rather dirty, but the second one. She enters, and bolts the door. She gives a sigh of relief. She does not feel the need to relieve herself: neither the need nor the desire. Yet she hurriedly removes her knickers, rumpling her skirt with its pattern of squares and diamonds as she does so.

She settles there to wait, but for a long while no pupil comes in. After missing the first two lessons because of the concert, the teachers must be more reluctant to allow any pupils to leave the room. But patience is without doubt the greatest virtue of anyone who waits, whether it be a night-watchman or an angler at a pond. María Teresa is nothing if not patient. She has always been that way. She waits completely patiently while nobody enters and nothing happens. Until at a certain moment, as she is studying the narrow gaps between the tiles of the toilet, she hears the unmistakable creak of the swing doors.

12

A pupil comes in to urinate: nothing new there. María Teresa readies herself to do what she has become accustomed to do. Naked (naked beneath her skirt) she is ready to urinate at the same time as the pupil. This time, however, something stops her. At first, she herself cannot work out what it is. She has to pause and consider what is going on before she finally understands. It is not something she hears, or senses: it is something she smells. Something that smells on the boy who has come in. It was not there before, and now it is: that means there can be no doubt it is the pupil who has brought the smell in with him. She does not even have to ask herself what it is: it is the scent of Colbert cologne. Men's Colbert cologne, the one that comes in a glass bottle inside a green box. She knows what this scent is like; by now she would be able to tell it apart from dozens of others, as if this was a wine-tasting and she were an oenological expert. She can recognise this scent among many others, and it is what has just reached her nostrils.

While the boy is fiddling with his clothing at the urinal, María Teresa asks herself the obvious question: if this pupil who has just entered the toilet is about to urinate and wears Colbert cologne, it is none other than Baragli. In fact, it is because of Baragli that she knows what Colbert cologne is, and what fragrance it has. That does not mean there is a logical imperative that if a pupil uses that cologne it must be Baragli, because any other boy at the school, or even any other pupil in third year class ten, could also use that cologne. Obviously, it does not have to be Baragli. Equally obviously, however, it *could* be Baragli. It does not have to be him, but it could be him. And whereas with all the other students she lacks any evidence that they may do so, with him, there is all-important proof: she knows for certain that he does use Colbert cologne. With him it is more than a probability, it is a certainty.

María Teresa can bear many things, but this gnawing uncertainty is not one of them. She is pleased with the bold steps she has taken recently: getting into this toilet, staying so vigilant. She thinks this boldness is necessary to fulfil her declared aim of discovering the pupils who are smoking at school. Driven on by what she sees as a similar impulse, she now takes a bigger, even bolder step. She can no longer, it is true, consider it as an integral part of her strategy of surveillance, but she adopts it with the same determined assurance.

With fingers as nimble as those of a surgeon or watch-maker, she draws back the bolt on the cubicle door. The door is now open. She lets go of it and allows it to swing gently inwards. Now she is able to spy through a crack. Now she prepares to truly spy. Now she is literally going to spy on someone. The ajar door not only allows her to do so, it almost demands it. She does not consider the danger she is in, or disregards it. She only wants one thing: to peep through the gap. She wants to see which boy has entered the toilet and unzipped his trousers. She wants to see who it is. She wants to see if it is Baragli. There is a gap of only ten centimetres between the door and the frame. Just enough for her to put her face to it and look. A crack to which she can only press one edge of her anxious face. As she does so, she holds her breath. She wants to be more than stealthy: she wants to be invisible. And being invisible, to see. She presses her cheek against the door, is invisible, and sees: she sees the boy who has just come into the toilet and at that very moment is starting to urinate. He does this of course into the urinal, and therefore has his back to her. But not completely. Since he is using the first one, the one closest to the swing doors, he is at a relatively wide angle to the cubicles. Basically with his back to them, but partly in profile.

María Teresa looks, and it is not Baragli. That much is obvious. Baragli is taller than this boy, his back is broader and his hair is fairer. It is not Baragli. It is another boy. Another boy, but still a boy.

A pupil at the school who has come into the toilet to urinate. María Teresa watches him from her hiding place. It is not one of the boys from class ten either, the one she is in charge of. As far as she can tell, it is a boy from class seven, a boy she has often noticed, although she has no idea of his name. The boy urinates. She can see the back of his head, the light-blue collar of his uniform shirt, the stripes of the blue blazer down his back. She can see his grey trousers, which hang down slightly due to the simple fact that they are undone. She can see him urinating. Sees him urinate. She also sees part of his profile: an ear, some of his face, now and then the tip of his nose. She can see the way his right arm is thrust forward. Above all, she can see the jet of urine splashing against the urinal, then curling its way downwards. The pupil's head is pointing down too, because he is watching himself urinate. He must be seeing his thing, seeing the urine cascade out of it. She, María Teresa, the assistant of third year class ten, watches him urinate and watches him watching himself. After a few seconds, the flow of urine starts to diminish. She can tell by the amount falling and by the angle at which it falls. Then the flow stops. It seems as though this is the end, but just as that moment there is something like a colophon, an addition, a supplement: three or four more spurts, shorter than the original but no less strong, deliberately aimed by the pupil, thanks to a clever manipulation of his thing. María Teresa wonders whether she should withdraw into her cubicle and even, if it is not too dangerous, draw the bolt again. Something tells her, however, not to do so, but to wait: to go on spying a little longer. Unlike girls, boys when they have finished do not wipe or dry themselves, unless they have a problem; instead they shake their thing. María Teresa confirms this now; she sees the arm move, and the hand. As he does so, the boy turns his whole body slightly to one side, and so is more sideways on to her. María Teresa sees, at the end of the hand, that thing that boys have: a man's thing. If she sees it, she sees it being shaken; but possibly she only deduces this. She would like to make sure, but that is impossible. She thinks she sees it, and now that the pupil is putting it away, it should be said that to some extent she thinks she has seen it. But if she had to describe it (and although it may seem surprising, however giddy María Teresa feels, she manages to ask herself how she would describe what she saw or believes she has seen), she would not know how to. She does not think a young woman like her would ever have the kind of conversation where this would come up. Instead, she imagines what words she would use to describe to someone what that thing she saw or thought she saw is like, and she cannot find any. None, nothing at all, her mind is a blank. And yet she would swear, if something of this kind could ever require an oath, that she really did see the boy's thing.

She pulls back and pushes the door to. After he has done up his trousers, the boy could turn round completely to go and wash his hands. He does not do so, however, but leaves the toilet straightaway. María Teresa stays a little longer sheltered in the cubicle, with the door still slightly ajar. All at once she realises she is kneeling. She goes over everything that happened in her mind, as though it were a film whose plot she has to summarise. Recovering from her confusion, she stands up, takes the rolled-up toilet paper from her pocket and then, raising her skirt, leans over and wipes herself, without noticing or remembering that this time she has not done anything.

On the following days she resists the temptation to spy on the urinals with the door open. She dimly acknowledges that in doing so she is admitting she has considered the possibility that there is a point at which she might do it again. If she does not do so, it is because she recognises the danger as too great. She prefers not to run this risk, or rather she prefers to keep it in reserve, as if it were a scarce resource she does not want to waste, for a very special occasion which may soon occur: that a boy comes into the toilet, the air fills with a definite scent she will immediately recognise as Colbert cologne, and that boy is Baragli. Baragli and no-one else. Possibly when that happens she will do what she recently did: open the door a few centimetres and peer out. In an obscure way, she senses that if she does this each time a pupil comes in, she is reducing the possibility that on some occasion, some afternoon, it will be Baragli.

At break-time, in the quad she often runs into the boy from class seven whom she saw in the toilet. Whenever this happens, she cannot help but watch what he is doing, and even sometimes follow him (the boy goes to the tuck shop, buys a chocolate biscuit, then renews his conversation with a couple of friends). She finds it better to follow him than to look straight at him, because that way she recognises the back of his neck and the curve of his back. What she sees and what she saw mingle in a pleasurable sensation. She hears the others call him Subán. That must be his name then: Subán. Until now she had not known what he was called, and yet she had seen him, she had seen it. He joins other pupils, becomes part of a laughing group. From a distance, María Teresa watches the casual way he waves his hand about; eventually she tears herself away and returns to her duties as an assistant in other parts of the quad.

For several days her surveillance in the boys' toilet reveals nothing new. It is plain how powerful the force of habit is: sooner or later, almost everything succumbs to it. The pupils come in and out as always, urinate or defecate, sometimes they also spit, wash their faces or hands, comb or muss up their hair in front of the mirror. What they do not do is smoke: for the moment none of them has come in for this reason, and that continues to be the case.

María Teresa has become so used to taking up her position that during break-time, when the toilet fills with pupils coming in and out, she gets the strange impression that a very personal space of her own is being invaded. Over the weeks, things have become reversed: she is not the intruder in the boys' toilet, but they are: the pupils, the boys, the ones who only spend a moment in a place which for her has become somewhere long-lasting, permanent; boys who after all are only paying a fleeting visit to a place which for her is somewhere she inhabits, a bit like the residents of a tourist destination over-run by visitors during the holiday season.

On exceptional occasions, two boys come into the toilet together during lesson time. By definition they cannot be from the same class, because no teacher would ever allow two pupils to leave the classroom at the same time (nor do they ever permit a boy and a girl to leave, even if they are going to different toilets, because that would mean they walked together unaccompanied along the school cloisters, and that is something to be prevented at all costs). If two pupils arrive together at the boys' toilet it must be because by pure chance they asked to leave their classrooms at the same time. They meet either in the corridor or as they are going into the toilet; they may ignore each other and not say a word, or they might, even if they are not friends and hardly know each other, take advantage of their chance meeting to strike up a conversation.

Whenever this happens, María Teresa makes sure she listens to what the pupils say when they are alone, or think they are. Usually, they talk about their teachers (the ones giving them lessons at the time), either to complain or poke fun at them. They also sometimes talk dirty, in the typical male conversations that María Teresa is familiar with despite herself, because her brother used to speak like that on the telephone with his friends without lowering his voice. They say, for example, that the woman teacher who takes them for geography must not be getting a fuck, or not a proper one: María Teresa listens to everything, offended by their swearing, but also concerned at the feverish fantasies boys of that age have, the way they think these matters are so easy to spot, as if there were no such thing as privacy or discretion. Fortunately, it is not often that two boys enter together, because the likelihood is rare that the teachers will let pupils out simultaneously, especially since they do not permit anyone to leave during the first twenty minutes of a class ('you've just had a break, you should have thought of it then') or during the last twenty ('restrain yourself, there's a break soon').

It occurs to María Teresa that when two boys are in the toilet together they are more likely to smoke, because in this kind of childish transgression there is a great degree of showing off: each of them wants to prove he is smarter than the other. Nothing of the sort ever happens, however, even when two of the pupils are in the toilet together. They may mention grotesque details of things they do or imagine, such obscene things María Teresa wipes them from her memory the moment she hears them, things that lead her to worry about the state of moral degeneration of boys that age. But, despite all her efforts, lighting a cigarette and smoking it is a breach of the rules she has still not encountered.

On afternoons when the invisible sky beyond the school

walls is covered with dove- or stone-grey clouds, the light inside the school dims still further. These are days when there are storms, although in the classrooms there is no way of knowing if in the life of the city outside it is already raining or not. In the cloisters and classrooms it is as if night were falling. However, it does not always become dark enough for the caretakers to decide to switch on the electric lights. Sometimes the lessons take place in a heavy atmosphere of murky gloom. On days like these, the already inadequate light filtering through the high, frosted windows into the toilet becomes so faint that only outlines can be made out. This increases María Teresa's sense that the boys' toilet is a kind of refuge. And the cubicle in which she chooses to shut herself each time is a refuge within a refuge. Naturally, this is due mostly to the fact that she feels she is in a position of absolute control, while at the same time never forgetting the risks she is running. Even so, whenever she enters a cubicle, she feels the sense of protection of a real refuge. The reason is simple enough: as soon as she is in the toilet she feels good, whether or not she was having a good day beforehand, or whether or not she is likely to have one after she leaves.

On the days when there are lowering clouds and the sky is covered (which are very frequent at this time of the year and in this part of autumn), when twilight spreads to every corner of the school, María Teresa is doubly conscious of the feeling that by hiding in the toilet she is protecting herself. She could swear that on days like these, when what the eyes can make out is limited, she hears better and her sense of smell is sharper. The same is said of the blind, if such a comparison can be made: that being deprived of one of their senses, all the others become more acute.

In her corner of the cubicle in the boys' toilet, María Teresa can hear every sound, even when they come from outside. It is a rainy day, and seems later than it really is (at three o'clock it seems like five o'clock, at four it is like six in the evening). She hears the swing doors creak, telling her someone is coming in. Yet the sounds that should follow are missing: footsteps inside the toilet, clothing being loosened, a sigh or a cough, breathing. None of this can be heard. María Teresa deduces that nobody came into the toilet, that what must have happened was that for some unknown reason a boy came to the toilet door, and then left. Left without coming in. She is busy pondering this when she hears the sound of the swing doors again, this time from the far end of the toilet. But it is not the usual sound, the rhythmic creak of the swing doors gradually subsiding, but a sound that starts, then suddenly stops. That can mean only one thing: that someone is holding the door, in order to look inside.

María Teresa thinks that whoever it may be will see there is nobody in the toilet and will disappear the way they came. She waits for this to happen, but the silence of the door being held extends longer than expected, which means the person checking that there is no-one in the toilet is taking great care over doing so. Just in case, she holds her breath. At last she hears the door being released: whoever was holding it has let go, so that it swings to and fro as it usually does. María Teresa sighs with relief, thinking the search must have concluded and that the person carrying it out has moved away.

Just at that moment, however, she hears footsteps close

to her, inside the toilet. Unhurried steps, the feet coming down firmly with each stride: the steady walk of someone inspecting a place. They do not head straight for the urinals, as anyone who had come to urinate would do, nor for one of the cubicles, as anyone who had come for something else would. They do not aim for anywhere in particular, but walk round the toilet in an initial reconnoitre.

More than ever before, María Teresa anxiously checks the distance between the floor and the bottom of the cubicle door. The gap is wide enough for anyone who is looking to be able to spot a pair of feet. She cowers back to try to avoid this happening. She no longer minds pressing against the far wall, which is often splashed and dirty, or having to tread on the wet ceramic base with its black hole. None of this is as bad as being seen by someone looking under the cubicle door.

The footsteps move away. They sound firm once more as now they head for the urinals, but not to use them: it is clear that is not the point, but that this is another part of the close inspection. A few seconds later, the steps cross to the line of urinals at the opposite end of the toilet. When María Teresa hears them passing in front of her door, she instinctively stands on tiptoe, as though that would make them more invisible than two whole feet. If she could levitate, she would do so now: float in the air to avoid being seen by any eyes peering under the door. There is no need: the footsteps move on again. They reach the urinals on the other side. There is a pause, a very short one. The urinals are easy to check, all they require is a quick glance.

For no real reason, María Teresa is confident the inspection will end with this fleeting look at the urinals.

That is her hope, but there is no substance to it. What could anyone be looking for only in that area, and not in the rest of the boys' toilet? She does not know, has no idea. That is not what happens anyway. The footsteps leave the urinals and head towards the door of the first cubicle. It is closed, but not bolted, because there is no-one inside. A strong hand pushes it open so hard the door bounces off the side partition and returns more or less to its original position. The steps enter the cubicle, only to exit again after a brief moment. Then they move on to the second cubicle. Here, the door is open. One step is enough to get inside and give a quick glance to see there is nothing to report. The third cubicle also has its green door closed (closed, but not bolted). This time it is opened less violently, so there is no sound of wood crashing against the wall. This toilet is not clean. María Teresa knows that, because she looked in and rejected it before choosing the fourth cubicle, the one next to it, where she is now. It is not clean: all round the drain hole are pieces of thrown-away toilet paper and the traces of a rushed evacuation. There is a sort of groan, followed by a muttered curse. Whoever is complaining does what she herself did not do, what she could not have done without giving away her illicit presence. She hears the chain being pulled and the water flushing. The first noise is a metallic click, the second sounds like the speeded-up, abbreviated recording of a waterfall. The footsteps move out of the third cubicle. The fourth is bound to be next, because everything about the inspection is being done methodically. María Teresa is in the fourth cubicle. The green door is not only shut, it is bolted, because inside the fourth cubicle is the assistant of the third year class ten.

Trembling, terrified, wishing she did not exist, unable to believe what is happening. The person inspecting does not know this. He knows the door is closed. He does not know it is bolted, but can see it is closed, because after a short detour the footsteps come to a halt right in front of it. The hand tries to push the door open, as with the previous ones. But nothing happens. The door does not open. The hand pushes more firmly, suspecting it might be stuck due to dried paint or swollen wood. But neither of these is the problem. The door does not move because it is locked, bolted. So the person inspecting the toilet now knows that in addition to being shut, the door is bolted. And he knows that the only explanation for this is that there must be someone inside. María Teresa feels the urge to urinate, this time out of fear.

13

Above all, no fuss. Discreet, gentle taps with the knuckles on the green door of the fourth cubicle. Nothing worse than to upset the poor boy who might have diarrhoea (only that could lead him not to wait until he got home) perching precariously over the hole with his trousers round his knees.

But there is no reply.

There are a further four or five knocks, still discreet but louder now. More urgent, demanding an answer. María Teresa cannot give one. She cannot even whisper a brief 'occupied', because she would have to say it in her female voice, or worse still, try to imitate a boy's voice, which would only be bound to precipitate the disaster.

So she decides to remain completely silent. Perhaps that will save her. But it does not: against the silence she so stubbornly clings to another voice can be heard. A man's voice, a voice not unknown to her.

—Name, year, and form.

María Teresa is dumb, remains dumb.

The voice insists, peremptory now.

—Name, year, and form.

María Teresa cannot reply. She says nothing.

The voice becomes harsher.

—Name! Year! Form!

The voice is so violent it only intimidates her still further. Silence is her only defence, her only hope. To stay silent, until the questioner grows tired and leaves the toilet. He might eventually think that on the other side of the bolted door there is simply a boy dying of shame to be caught with diarrhoea. If so, the voice will eventually give up and go away. For a brief moment, she hopes this is what is going to happen, because the voice stops asking questions and disappears.

This could be the outcome she so fervently desires. But it is not. It is exactly the opposite: a prelude, a gathering of momentum. The prelude to a totally unexpected event.

A brutal blow descends on the wooden door. It quakes, like a person punched in the stomach. It does not collapse or splinter, but reveals its essential fragility. The door is made of thin, light wood that is not very tough, and consists of vertical panels which bend with the blow and show the joins. There is a second thump, and this is enough to break it down. Strictly speaking, it is not the door that gives way, but the bolt. Not the wooden panels, but the badly screwed-in metal fitting and the steel bolt itself. This is completely torn off, snapped apart with a noise like something crunching. In a second, the flimsy mechanism is reduced to its basic elements: a strip of metal, a small steel bar, three screws (one was already missing).

The door opens.

It is as if it opens on its own, or gives that impression, because the blow merely shattered the bolt rather than opening the door. This opening happens independently, because the bolt is no longer there, and for this reason it occurs slowly, and takes a long time to be complete. The door swings back in slow motion, and the double revelation is equally slow. Inside, María Teresa's blood runs cold when she sees Señor Biasutto's unmistakable outline. Outside, Señor Biasutto clenches his teeth, peers in, and finally sees who it is.

The echo of his blows on the door has completely died away.

There is no sign of astonishment on Señor Biasutto's tense face. There is no expression at all. But it must be astonishment, if not complete consternation, which at first prevents him from being able to utter a word. Several long seconds go by, with María Teresa trying hard not to burst into tears.

Señor Biasutto finally says something, barely opening his mouth.

—What are you doing here?

María Teresa struggles to hold back a knot of tears and saliva choking her.

—My job.

Señor Biasutto's tiny black eyes open wider.

—Your job? What do you mean by that?

María Teresa cringes back still further against the filthy wall.

—Señor Biasutto, I am supervising the behaviour and respect for the regulations of the pupils at this school.

Señor Biasutto nods several times, as though he finally grasps what is going on, but the way he spreads both hands out by his sides suggests he has not really understood anything.

—What behaviour or respect for regulations could you possibly be supervising in here?

164

María Teresa no longer feels she is about to burst into tears. Señor Biasutto is at least giving her the chance to explain.

—You remember I once told you of my suspicions about pupils smoking at school?

—Yes, I remember.

—And since that kind of breach of the regulations is typical of rebellious boys, it was easy to conclude that the place where they committed this infraction was in their toilet.

—Very well . . .

—Well then, that is why I am here. I hide to see if I can catch anyone smoking.

Señor Biasutto thinks this over for a while.

—Here, among all the shit and piss?

María Teresa nods.

—Yes.

Señor Biasutto reconsiders his position. He does so mentally, but also physically: dropping his hands to his sides, he steps back a metre or two. This is his way of inviting María Teresa to come forward out of the stinking hole, but she is still too terrified to move.

—Come on, come out of there.

The lack of light in the toilet suddenly makes the scene less dramatic.

—Listen to me: come out now.

María Teresa staggers out of the cubicle as if she had spent three months in bed convalescing from some serious illness and this was the moment to get up and see if she still had any feeling in her legs.

—Come and wash your hands.

As soon as Señor Biasutto mentions her hands, she suddenly realises that all this time she has been clutching her pair of knickers. She has become so used to taking them off in the cubicle she does it every time she enters in. It is a plain white pair, with none of the frilly lace of some others she has. Señor Biasutto does not seem to have noticed anything; possibly he has not seen them, or perhaps thought they were something else. She takes advantage of him turning towards the wash-basins to stuff the knickers between her pullover and skirt. She is uncomfortable about not having anything on underneath, but there is no alternative. Señor Biasutto turns on one of the taps and encourages her to come over, as if this were a cold buffet at a party and he was inviting her to try a special delicacy. The running water combines with the dim light to create a sense of calm. Pushing up her sleeves to avoid getting them wet, María Teresa starts to wash her hands. She rubs the oval of soap until there are some suds, and afterwards carefully rinses her hands. Señor Biasutto watches this process carefully, as though she were a little girl at a mischievous age who might try to avoid washing, and he were her father making sure she did it properly.

Once she has finished it becomes obvious she has nowhere to dry her hands. There are no towels or paper rolls. To María Teresa's relief, Señor Biasutto reacts with his customary gallantry, pulling a yellow handkerchief from the breast pocket of his dark blue jacket. Perfectly folded, the handkerchief matches his tie and socks (although she does not find out about the socks). He hands it to her, leaning forward slightly. She takes it with thanks. It is not made of cotton, but of silk or some synthetic fibre, which means it does not dry very well; in spite of this she feels truly grateful. She finishes drying her hands, or spreading the damp around a little, then gives the handkerchief back to Señor Biasutto. He refuses to accept it.

—That's all right, you can keep it.

She is secretly delighted at the idea of keeping one of Señor Biasutto's handkerchiefs. She refolds it into four and pushes it up her sleeve. The courtesies continue: Señor Biasutto steps forward again, but this time it is to hold open one of the swing doors for María Teresa.

—After you.

They walk almost alongside each other down the cloister leading to the assistants' room. They do not speak. Señor Biasutto's silence seems to stem from a pensive reflection on what he has seen; María Teresa, on the other hand, is still in the grip of fear. She would like him to say something more, something that she could clearly interpret as his verdict. But he does not deliver it. He does not say a word. He walks along, hands clasped behind his back, staring at the ground where he is about to step. His attitude is characteristic of somebody lost in thought, but María Teresa has no idea what he might be thinking.

The school day ends without any repercussion. Nor is there any in the days that follow. María Teresa is relieved to find that Señor Biasutto has not taken any action against her. He has not made any report to the Head of Discipline, or worse still to the Deputy Headmaster. This must mean he does not disapprove of her initiative. He has done nothing; he has not sought any punishment. He would surely have done so without the slightest hesitation if he had thought it necessary. Judging him to be a completely upright man, María Teresa dismisses the idea he could have been lenient towards her: it would never even have occurred to him to cover or protect her. If he has not imposed any sanctions (which could have been anything from a verbal warning to dismissal) it must be because he does not openly disapprove of her actions.

However, the situation he found her in was so ambiguous, so similar to what she was hoping for with the pupils: to catch them *in flagrante*, that she no longer feels she can continue with the task she has set herself. She does not go back into the boys' toilet. Although Señor Biasutto did not openly disapprove, meaning perhaps he was giving his tacit approval, he did not encourage her when he saw what she was getting into (shit, he said, using male language) in order to carry out her duties as assistant even more effectively. Since that is how things stand, it seems to her only obvious to completely suspend her surveillance.

She therefore returns to what was more strictly speaking her work routine. She spends more time in the assistants' room. None of the others make any comment about this, doubtless because none of her colleagues are interested enough in her to note any difference. Of course, the school days are much duller. Life was never full of passion for her, but she now finds herself increasingly bored. The reason to get up each morning has disappeared, and this has had a serious effect on her state of mind. It is true, however, that it gives her the opportunity to see Señor Biasutto more frequently. The assistants' supervisor works chiefly in the room where they all meet whilst teachers are taking lessons. María Teresa is now able to see and deal with him more often. Yet she senses he is more distant. She attributes this to the fact that the great hope she had regarding him no longer exists: to astound him by uncovering the pupils smoking on the sly at school. Her dream had been that this was what would truly consolidate their relationship. She now realises that since she has abandoned her close surveillance, this hope has evaporated. Furthermore, the other possibility she was looking forward to, that of meeting him again in a café after work, has also become more problematical. It is as though the first contact established between them at the end of their first encounter, which she sees as a bridge, had come crashing down, as a result of the episode in the boys' toilet. There is no sign that Señor Biasutto might consider asking her to meet a second time. As the days go by, the faint echoes of their first meeting die away, and soon it will seem (if this is not already the case) that it never happened.

Meanwhile, more postcards arrive from Francisco in Comodoro Rivadavia. There are two of them, showing aerial views: so high in the sky in fact that they must have been taken from an aircraft in flight. The sharp outline of the coast is visible against the sea and the dense blue of the waveless waters, so dark it is a kind of gun-metal blue (or oil blue, thinks María Teresa, even though she doubts if that is a real word or if she simply thinks that because she knows there are lots of oilfields in that region of Argentina). The sea looks quiet. It is not lively, like the beaches on cards from Mar del Plata, for example, which conjure up images of fun and leisure. No, it is quiet, and not because of the effects of the photograph: it is quiet and dark like secrets that will never be revealed. For his part, the brother no longer writes anything: he leaves the reverse side of the cards completely blank. Nothing is written there, not even his name.

Developments at school during these days are as follows: the Head of Discipline has called all the assistants together to tell them that now more than ever they need to keep a sharp eye on the wearing of patriotic rosettes; Servelli laughed when Miss Pesotto had a sudden sneezing fit, and was given a double warning; Capelán has grown and Rubio has not, and therefore Rubio is at the front of the line-up of boys; Rubio has given no sign of using Marré as anything other than a point from which to take distance; Mr Roel is ill and will not be in for half a week, round-neck pullovers are forbidden, and this should be added to the regulations (until now it was taken for granted that all pullovers were V-necked); Costa's ribbon fastening at the top of her blouse has snapped, and she is using this as an excuse to leave the top button undone and show her neck, something she is strictly forbidden to do; a last-minute power failure has prevented the recording of 'Aurora' being played, so that at the end of school the pupils have to sing the anthem *a capella*, leading to a great deal of tuneless singing and some hesitation over the words; Bosnic's hair is too long and must be cut; Babenco was caught chewing gum; Dreiman ties her hair so low down it is almost as though it were loose, and should be warned; the blackboards in third year class ten have started to squeak when they are raised or lowered, and the janitor needs to be informed.

Their free music lesson is taken up with a showing of a film related to their syllabus (a version of Mozart's *The Magic Flute*). This makes it necessary to accompany the pupils to the small cinema in the basement. The basement makes María Teresa feel uneasy again, aware as she is of the secret tunnels leading off from there. Stories are told about them (it is impossible for there to be secret tunnels without stories being told): from nefarious excursions of priests at the adjacent church, to subterranean escapes during the English invasions of Buenos Aires at the beginning of the nineteenth century. There is also talk of a bombing plot that failed a few years earlier, although some say this plot never existed, and use the word 'excuse' to refute it. María Teresa does not know much about any of this: she knows there are priests who commit sins; she knows that the English invaders were valiantly repelled by throwing cauldrons of boiling water on them from the rooftops; she knows that a few years before now if you saw any suspicious package in the street, you had at all costs to avoid touching it. None of this is the source of her concern about the tunnels: it is their mere existence that troubles her. Not what might have happened in them, but the very fact that, beneath what is known and visible, there are passageways that are part of a realm that cannot be known or seen. Occasionally she is tempted to peer into one of them, although she would never actually dare enter them. This region of dank walls and rats frightens her, with a fear that struggles with the sense of mystery she finds attractive, but which in no way diminishes her unease.

It is a long, slow-moving film. The pupils follow it closely. Just in case, from his sick bed Mr Roel has telephoned to warn them that one of the three questions they will have in their next music written test will refer to the film. María Teresa sporadically checks on the class's behaviour. Everything seems to be as it should be, and the lesson ends without a hitch. When the lights come up again, it is like the end of a hypnosis session.

The pupils line up to leave the room. They are not allowed out into the cloisters except in line and walking in an orderly fashion. María Teresa stands behind them, taking up the best position to see what they are doing without being seen. Because of this however, as the pupils file out of the cinema she is the last to see that Señor Biasutto is waiting in the doorway. There is no reason for her to be surprised that the supervisor should be there, and yet she is slightly shocked. When a class has a lesson outside their routine (which this film screening in the basement definitely is) it is normal for him to come and make sure there are no problems (there is a double purpose to this: on the one hand, his presence can be seen as support for whichever assistant is involved; on the other, it is his way of keeping an eye on that assistant: making sure that they are looking after things properly).

—Everything all right?

María Teresa replies without looking directly at him.

—Yes, fine.

—Is this a music lesson?

—Yes, it's their music class. Mr Roel is off sick.

Señor Biasutto nods and falls in beside María Teresa. The pupils are even better-behaved now that the supervisor is with them. They climb the stairs more or less in step, then walk along the corridor without dragging their feet, something that is not easily achieved with these reluctant pupils.

Although there are only a few minutes before the bell goes for break-time, the pupils of third year class ten enter their classroom. However still and silent they might be, they could not possibly stay out in the cloister while the rest of the school were in lessons. They walk in lined-up, first the girls, then the boys, and all sit down at their desks. There is no time for them to start anything. If they wanted to do anything, the time would be short. But it is long to spend it doing nothing: not talking or moving, staring into space at nothing in particular.

María Teresa has to go straight into the classroom to stand in front of the class and make sure this absence of activity is respected. Just as she is about to do so, Señor Biasutto halts her by laying a finger or two on her forearm. She turns towards him, and sees him blink.

—Any news about that idea of yours?

Bewildered, María Teresa raises a hand to her mouth.

—My idea?

Señor Biasutto nods.

—Yes. That idea about boys who smoke, who you are going to catch.

María Teresa takes the question as a compliment. Her reply is nervous, but pleased.

—No news as yet. Nothing for the moment.

As she enters the classroom she is happy, although she is careful to conceal her change of mood from the pupils. She takes what Señor Biasutto has said to her for what it undoubtedly is: the authorization to continue her surveillance in the boys' toilet; and the encouragement (clearly announced, if not emphasised) for her not to stop doing so.

14

And so she returns, as soon as she can, to take up her position in the cubicle. She has not missed many days. Only a few, in fact: three or four, although they passed by very slowly for her. For this reason, when she goes back to her post it is as though she were returning home or to her neighbourhood after being away on a lengthy journey (once, when she was a girl, after spending a month in a tiny village in Córdoba province, she found it hard to readjust to seeing traffic lights in the streets, and having a telephone at home). In the boys' toilet she sees signs of her absence, as though not simply by being somewhere, but also by not being there we leave behind certain personal traces.

Not for an instant does the possibility occur to her that the pupils may have been smoking in the toilet while she was not keeping an eye on it. It never even enters her head. In a reversal that she herself, if she were to think about it, would find illogical, María Teresa tends to believe breaking the rules in this way would be impossible if she, their personification, were not present. For her, it was not just her surveillance in the boys' toilet that was suspended for a few days, but everything involved and springing from that initiative. All that world, a confused mixture of mischief, rebellion, and the restoration of order, is reborn specifically for her, and precisely because she is returning; it has even taken on an extra dimension, since from now on her presence will not be that of a mere assistant, but can count on the express approval of Señor Biasutto, the supervisor.

Such is her enthusiasm when she slips back into the boys' toilet for the first time that she is not in the least frustrated that no-one comes to use the facilities (either for their proper purpose or for illicit use), in the same way as when all this began. Now more than ever, reflecting on the interest that Señor Biasutto has shown, María Teresa is absolutely certain that if she is in the cubicle, sooner or later the pupils who smoke at school will come in and do so, and she will catch them red-handed.

Something, however, does change in her behaviour after this brief hiatus. She no longer wants to relieve herself in this unsuitable place; nor does she, perhaps as a consequence, remove any of her clothes while she is in the cubicle. She only does the essential: she barricades herself in and keeps a lookout. She is determined to do nothing apart from be there and wait until the moment arrives for her to leap into action. She is not upset at this retreat. At most, it somewhat diminishes her, but she is not capable of seeing this about herself. Her thoughts are as restricted as she now is. She waits, nothing more than that. She does not get her hopes up with every boy who enters, and so is not constantly disappointed. She waits patiently, but not anxiously. Nothing is gained by expecting too much. No point rushing things. What has to happen will happen in due course.

It is ten days before the start of winter, but Buenos Aires seems to have left behind all lingering traces of autumn. The weather is very cold. The school buildings were designed to provide sufficient shelter to make study possible, but nothing more: too much comfort would eventually lead to less concentration on learning. The use of gloves and scarves is permitted outside the school, provided they are blue in colour (the same blue as their pullovers, not any other sort), but they have to be taken off and put away before entering the premises. Wearing berets or woolly caps is forbidden both inside and outside the school, because they look untidy.

The toilets are colder than the cloisters, and the cloisters colder than the classrooms. Today the pupils go out in turn into the inner quad, that is into the open air, to practise marching, because the commemoration of Manuel Belgrano, ex-pupil and creator of the national flag, is fast approaching. Mr Vivot shouts out instructions (leff, righ, leff, attenshun, at eeasse!) through a megaphone that gives everything a metallic echo. A cloud of condensation appears on the pupils' lips, caused by the cold, or more exactly by the sudden contact of their warm breath with the cold air. Something similar happens in the toilet. Not in the cloisters, still less in the classrooms, but definitely in the toilets. Each puff of breath produces a hazy white cloud.

María Teresa notices this phenomenon, which proves to her it really is cold and that it is not because she is not warmly enough dressed. Somebody enters the toilet, walking quickly. He does not head for the urinals, but comes directly towards the cubicles. And not to any of them, but straight to the only one that is shut, the one she is waiting in.

There is a gentle tap on the door, like someone who wants to enter a bedroom where one person is asleep and another awake, and knocks so that the person awake will hear and the person asleep will not be woken. María Teresa hears the knock. Obviously she does not reply. As on the previous occasion, she withdraws to the far end of the cubicle. She does not reply, and has no intention of doing so.

Knowing this, Señor Biasutto whispers.

—Open up, María Teresa, it's me.

She draws back the bolt and opens the door. Señor Biasutto smiles at her, although she cannot interpret its meaning. Possibly she sees one of his nostrils palpitating. His hands are clasped again, this time in front of him.

—Any developments?

A routine check, as the doctors say. Señor Biasutto, supervisor of the school's assistants, is inspecting the work of a member of the team he is in charge of.

—Nothing for the moment, Señor Biasutto.

Señor Biasutto makes a gesture, possibly with a finger, towards the interior of the cubicle. He is still smiling, but the movement is one of command.

—For a woman, you make a good watchman.

She does not entirely understand what he means by this, but it seems better to accept and agree rather than to ask him to explain.

—I'm simply doing my duty.

Señor Biasutto nods encouragingly, but almost at once his features crease in an unaccustomed frown, and his eyebrows start to twitch. Eventually, as though trying to recover from this sudden bout of anxiety, he smiles and shrugs his shoulders, rumpling his jacket. Then, his

177

mind made up, without asking permission (there is no reason he should: he is the assistants' supervisor, after all) he takes a step, so big it amounts to a long stride, until he is entirely inside the cubicle. María Teresa thinks she should consider this as him coming to take over from her: she is convinced that Señor Biasutto is so committed to the investigation she is carrying out that he has come to replace her. She therefore makes to leave the cubicle and the toilet altogether, moving forward in a measured but determined way. With a simple push of the hand, Señor Biasutto shuts the door. Shuts it and immediately bolts it. Now both of them, she and he, María Teresa the class assistant and Señor Biasutto, her supervisor, are locked in the boys' toilet. Obviously there is very little room for the two of them, even more so because neither of them wants to step on the lavatory itself, although this time it is not that dirty. There is no way they can avoid being squashed against each other. Señor Biasutto's thin moustache, which she now sees more clearly than ever, appears to acquire a life of its own. She presses herself against the partition, but that proves as useless as it would be between the rows of books in a library or archive. The furthest she can get away from him is still far too close. Far from being tall, Señor Biasutto is quite the opposite. In fact, he may be no taller than she is, or only a little taller. Despite this, she now finds herself peering up at him. He smiles at her. When he does this, there is a shine to his lips which must come from saliva. His teeth are covered this time, she cannot see them. María Teresa attempts to return his smile, but finds herself unable to. If she could escape the paralysis born of fear she would probably cry rather than smile.

She has no idea what is going to happen in here with Señor Biasutto. What she does realise in the midst of her confusion is that none of this has anything to do with trying to catch pupils breaking the school rules. It must be something else. María Teresa does not know what, but this much she does know. Señor Biasutto is as composed as ever: his smooth, brilliantined hair, straightened tie, shirt-collar without a single wrinkle, his jacket lapels immaculate; yet even so there is something dishevelled about him. María Teresa tries to calm down, repeating to herself what she already knows: that Señor Biasutto is the supervisor of the school's assistants, that his reputation among his colleagues is of the highest, that he is a man of the world, and that, as she has herself discovered, he can behave as a perfect gentleman towards women. She thinks about all this, knows it to be true, and yet none of it reassures her.

Señor Biasutto thrusts his arms forwards in his jacket sleeves, then undoes one of the buttons. That is all: he undoes a button. The jacket falls open, to reveal a white shirt. He is not wearing a pullover. That is all. Some people do not feel the cold. Some men never wear their jacket buttoned up. Perhaps now Señor Biasutto will feel more at ease, better able to put up with the lack of space. But no. Instead he thrusts his arms forward again several times, and his shoulders start to twitch once more. It is hard, if not impossible, to tell how old Señor Biasutto is. This is what María Teresa is thinking; she also wonders, aware that her mind is wandering, if he has another Christian name, and what month he was born in.

He takes her by the shoulders and turns her round. Firmly, insistently. She finds herself facing the tile-covered

179

wall, her face almost flattened against it. She can make out every detail: every slight discoloration, the smallest roughness. Some of the chill of the tiles spreads to her cheeks. Señor Biasutto is now directly behind her. María Teresa still manages to tell herself, for no apparent reason, that after all he is the supervisor of the class assistants at the National School of Buenos Aires.

Señor Biasutto fumbles with her skirt. As he lifts it, she feels the cold on her legs and starts to feel afraid. Unless he keeps hold of it with one hand, her skirt drops again, making Señor Biasutto even more awkward and frantic. Pulling her skirt back up, he sees her thighs, the outline of her concealed buttocks, but finds he needs both hands and so lets go of the material. He starts panting, struggles desperately with his own clumsiness. He is not expecting María Teresa to do anything, except to be there, his assistant, his subaltern, one side of her face pressed against the tiles. Finally he manages to undo himself, although he is still caught up in his trousers. Pushing up her skirt once more, he uses one hand to hold it up on her back. María Teresa feels his cold, damp fist on her; she remembers how when he said farewell that night on the street corner opposite the church Señor Biasutto bent forward, as if in the hall of a great palace, and brushed her fingertips with his lips. It was cold in Buenos Aires that night too.

With his free hand, Señor Biasutto tears down her knickers. Since he is only pulling on one side, the right-hand side, the knickers become twisted. He has to reach over with this hand, underneath the other one, to straighten them up. He does this with great difficulty. By now María Teresa's knickers are down round her knees, the elastic looser than when they were round her waist, where they ought to be worn and where they ought to be now. In pulling so roughly he has rolled them down, so that they look like sheets rolled by someone wanting to use them as a rope to escape out of a window. María Teresa's most intimate parts must now be on view.

María Teresa squints back at the bolt on the door. It is firmly locked. She wonders if the bolt in the other cubicle that broke when Señor Biasutto forced his way in a few days ago has been repaired.

She could have checked, but did not do so. It cannot have been very difficult to put the screws back in. They might even have replaced the missing one while they were at it. But if the wood was split when the metal fitting was torn from the door, it would not have been so easy to repair. Anyone using that cubicle to relieve themselves would find the door would not lock. If they had no time to change cubicles, they would have to try to keep their balance by putting one hand on the side wall, and stretch the other out in front of them to stop another unaware person coming in while they were in mid-flow. Why, for what reason, is María Teresa thinking things like this when the bolt of the cubicle where she is looks perfectly sound, and the door is locked? She can hear Señor Biasutto panting behind her. He pushes a hand inside her. Then he uses his other hand to help him, no longer worried that the skirt could fall again, because his arms will stop it anyway. One hand helping the other. One opens, the other pushes. María Teresa is terrified at the thought of Señor Biasutto's thing. She wills herself to look sideways and down. As yet Señor Biasutto's thing is not part of what is going on. As far as she can tell, it is still some way from her, and not responding. It is his hand that is doing everything, forcing its way inside her. A cold, clammy hand. The other one, just as cold and wet, is helping out. It pushes her flesh to one side and opens her up, makes it easier for the other hand to slide its way in. María Teresa cannot cry out or escape. She stares at the bolt: it is drawn, the door is locked. She is not thinking of opening it. No, that is not what she is thinking: she is remembering the brutal way in which the other bolt snapped off a few days earlier from the blows that Señor Biasutto rained down on the door. The screws shot out as if they had exploded, and the wood splintered all over the place. That is what she thinks as she sees the intact bolt behind her. She thinks of this and of Señor Biasutto's thing, which is not in sight: if only it stays that way.

She suffers the thrusting of his hands in silence. One hand plucks and pinches; the other simply thrusts. These actions are so blind and unfocused that it is hard to make out what their real intention is. She does what she can with her own hands: she spreads the palms against the smooth wall to stop the heaving behind her making her head hit the tiles. She cannot shout or moan. For some reason, her cautious instinct to go unnoticed in the toilet remains with her. She tightens her lips and clenches her teeth as she feels Señor Biasutto's dusty breath far too close to her ears and the back of her neck. The rummaging around continues for a while, apparently with no definite aim, until suddenly one of Señor Biasutto's hands, the most agile one, the one that has forced its way inside, changes direction. It changes like one of those strange tracked combat vehicles that can go immediately into reverse or swing to one side or another according to the demands of battle. Until now that hand was being used more or less as a fist, a bunch of clenched fingers, which did no more than push forward blindly. Now though one finger emerges from the rest, the middle finger: or perhaps it is better to say that four fingers withdraw, leaving this one to press home the attack. With a shudder, María Teresa again starts to think of Señor Biasutto's fearful thing, but she can see it is still apart from the fray. It is the wounding finger that is plunging deep inside her. A humiliating finger forcing its way in.

Afterwards, when she is able to, María Teresa will burst into tears over all this, but for the moment no tears come. To stay calm, she thinks: afterwards I will be able to cry, I will be able to shout. For now she clenches her teeth, screws up her eyes, tenses her hands, presses her whole body against the wall. Señor Biasutto stabs at her with his middle finger. To stay calm, María Teresa thinks: I am not losing my virginity. The finger penetrates her thirstily, greedily. Desperate, she thinks, tells herself: this does not mean I am no longer a virgin. Señor Biasutto's finger is not yet all the way inside her. He pulls it out a little, which hurts still more. Is he going to remove it altogether? No, he is not: he is merely gathering momentum. He pushes it back in as far as he can, as offensively as an insult. Afterwards, later that night when she is back at home, in her bed or under the shower she will want to take as soon as she arrives, she will be able to release the cry that is stuck in her throat now, the tears that are welling up in the corners of her eyes.

Nobody comes into the toilet, and that would be no use anyway. Señor Biasutto is in charge. He has stuck his finger in her. He plunges it inside and leaves it there: inside her.

All of a sudden he starts to moan. Señor Biasutto gives a thin, high-pitched moan that does not seem to come out of his mouth. Yet it does: it comes from his twisted, saliva-covered mouth. There is something not right about his teeth. It is as though he wanted to appropriate her pain, as if he can take over the expression of pain she cannot permit herself. He moans, snivels: she plucks up courage and glances back at him while he is beside himself in this way. She sees how his features are racked with sobs, how he is gripped by a strange suffering. His face is contorted, shiny with sweat. His moustache is like a scratch that has left a line of black blood above his crumpled mouth. Although his eyes are not shut, he cannot see anything. María Teresa looks directly at them and sees they are blind.

The finger inside her forces her to stay as still as she can. If she moves, it will only hurt more. She wonders how long this will go on, what the outcome will be. She knows from her brother how this ends. But the other, that thing down there, when will that be over? Señor Biasutto's face is continuously changing in ways she cannot interpret. Most of the grimaces seem to indicate pain. María Teresa observes him and waits, biting a finger of her own hand to help bear it. She no longer feels the cold.

The automatic flush goes off in the urinals. There is the sound of water gushing, falling, collecting. It goes off even when there is no-one there, and has a single function: to clear away any residues. On this occasion, however, it also does something more, unforeseen and in no way deliberate: it offers María Teresa a sign (which is also a relief) that the world outside still exists and is still going on, that she can return to it, that what is happening to her has not destroyed her, is not everything.

Señor Biasutto finally relaxes (his features and the whole of his body relax), and he decides to remove his finger. He pulls it straight out, as he had seemed to be doing before but did not complete. It hurts a lot, more than before, more than ever. It hurts. María Teresa moans for the first and only time: a faint, short moan. Señor Biasutto's finger is outside now, outside her. It is as if it is part of its master's hand once more: a released attack dog that now returns wearily to the pack.

María Teresa senses that relief may be on the way, but immediately shudders and wonders if the thought is something she cannot yet allow herself. The only one who knows what comes next is Señor Biasutto, with that enormous thing of his. He is the head of the assistants. She cannot cry out. It could be that at this very moment, just when she thinks the pain and the humiliation have finished, Señor Biasutto returns to the attack, and with nothing less than his fearful thing. Then all this will not be the end, it will only be the beginning.

But Señor Biasutto's thing remains as uninvolved as it was at the start. Nothing of what has happened seems directed towards it, or if it was it has taken no notice. Although she is terrified at the sight of it, it has not grown at all, has played no part. The finger-substitute is Señor Biasutto's last resort. Besides, now that he has pulled away from her, Señor Biasutto looks so dazed and unwell that it does not seem possible he could take any kind of initiative. His eyes slowly recover their link to the real world. As they do so, by chance they come into contact with María Teresa gazing at him: she quickly turns and stares ahead of her once more.

Señor Biasutto's face twists in yet another grimace, and he laughs the laugh of an idiot. This real or pretend idiocy is the safe-conduct that masks his desire for impunity. Or perhaps it is not even that: nothing more than a hidden truth that surfaces for a second. The effect is the same: Señor Biasutto withdraws. Hunched and silent, he makes to leave the cubicle. His hand is shaking, his fingers knot as he tries to draw back the bolt. He eventually succeeds, opens the door, leaves María Teresa still inside. She quickly pulls up her knickers and straightens her clothing. She will not leave until he has gone. He will only leave without her. Señor Biasutto does up his jacket, and his torso is forced lumpily back into shape. He regains the air of a supervisor. His face also recovers the composed look of a person in authority. He strides out of the toilet, stamping his feet as if he were marching rather than walking, as if he too were practising for the parade in honour of Manuel Belgrano. He pushes so hard at the swing doors that they continue to oscillate and creak far longer than usual. His footsteps resound along the corridor.

He has not washed his hands.

15

María Teresa no longer visits the boys' toilet at the school. She stops going there. She is busy with her duties as a class assistant, as hard-working and conscientious as ever. A whole day goes by without her going anywhere near the boys' toilet, but also without her even thinking about it. This is not like the previous occasion, when she did not go in there but was aware all the time that she was not doing so. Now she has given up on everything: doing what was once so important to her, and above all thinking about it. Her unconfessed wish is to alter the past, to delete what happened. It is not enough for her that it is no longer happening, or may not happen again: she needs it never to have happened. For this reason she does not even venture into the part of the cloister where the toilet is, and tries as far as possible to avoid the grim presence of Señor Biasutto.

The next day it is third year class ten's turn to practise parading round the quad outside the school library. María Teresa has to go with them to keep an eye on their behaviour, and so wraps up warm in a neutral-coloured woollen top her mother knitted for her at the start of the year. Two other classes from year three are also taking part in this rehearsal: class eight and class nine. Their assistants, Marcelo and Leonardo, also go out into the quad and exchange pleasantries with her as they keep watch unobtrusively.

The chief difficulty the pupils face is that they inevitably bend their knees with each stride. That is fine when they are walking, but not when they are marching. In order to march, they have to behave as though their knee joints were completely arthritic and stiff, and keep their legs straight, not bending them at all, jerking them forwards and backwards.

—You're not out for a stroll, ladies and gentlemen! This is a parade!

Despite the metallic echo from the megaphone, Mr Vivot's exasperation is plain for all to hear. Their legs should stay straight not only as they step forward, but when they are raised more than usual: this also causes problems (especially for the girls) because they tend to repeat the same movements they employ in normal life and cannot seem to understand that they are acquiring fresh skills.

—You're not in the park, ladies and gentlemen! You are in a parade!

They ought to think of the war films they all must have seen. If they concentrated on those they would respond better and satisfy Mr Vivot, who occasionally seems to be so enraged he will bite the end off his megaphone. Those war films clearly show what he is now trying to get the pupils to do: that from a side view like the one he adopts, all their legs and arms should always rise and fall together.

—As if you were one man, ladies and gentlemen! As if you were one!

He is doomed to failure. There is always one dunderhead who is either ahead or behind the rest, spoiling the rhythm.

He also has his work cut out trying to correct their habit of letting their arms hang by their sides. The pupils allow them to swing on their own, with their fingers also hanging down, instead of doing what Mr Vivot wants them to do: to hold their arms rigid and swing them vigorously (also to stop swinging them immediately, making sure they are not still waving about, when they have come to a halt).

—Don't walk, march! Don't walk! March!

The patriotic event will reach its climax with the swearing of the oath on the national flag. Could there be any more fitting homage to Manuel Belgrano, the man who created it? Argentinian children of the new generations, from the school for patriots he founded, will swear to give their lives for the flag. Their mothers almost always burst into tears at this point in the ceremony, while the fathers click away on their Kodak Instamatics, recording the scene for posterity. But the oath on the flag has also got to be rehearsed: it is not simply a matter of the pupils going up and saying, yes, they will die, they will give their lives for that flag, then muttering an oath, applause, and everyone on to the next thing. This is a solemn moment, comparable only to Christian baptism or communion, and it takes place around the hero's tomb. The pupils need to rehearse: eyes front means exactly that, none of them is to get distracted or so much as blink. An entire building could collapse on the pavement opposite them, but they are not to turn their heads for even a second, not even a centimetre. Eyes front means eyes front. And when the moment of swearing their oath to the flag comes, they all have to stare at the flag.

—Anyone I catch looking elsewhere can look for another school!

But worst of all would be if that swearing of the oath came out ragged or sounded unenthusiastic. Mr Vivot knows he already has enough on his hands trying to get the girls' voices to sound martial. He harangues all the pupils, with and without the megaphone. He asks them to consider the oath they are swearing: that they will honour the flag, give their lives for it. He asks them to respond from the heart, to feel in their souls what it means to be Argentinian. He gets them to practise.

—Yes, I swear!

—Again.

—Yes, I swear!

To make certain, Mr Vivot shouts encouragement; he tells them not to be so feeble, to be such namby-pambies. Loud and clear. Let the sound echo. Echo all round the quad. He seizes the megaphone. He chants the formula. He separates the words (that separation is vital: on no account must it seem as though they are simply swearing for its own sake, that they are responding automatically). He listens closely.

—Yes, I swear!

—Again.

—Yes, I swear!

—Once more.

—Yes, I swear!

—The last time!

—Yes, I swear!

Señor Biasutto appears at the door in the corner of the quad leading to the cloister. He appears interested in the parade rehearsal. He carefully checks the ends of each row of pupils, lends the sharpest of ears to the harmony of the collective oath-swearing. He goes over to Mr Vivot and exchanges a few words with him. From afar he waves to the assistants: Marcelo and Leonardo. To María Teresa as well. A brief but friendly gesture. Then he disappears back through the doorway where he first appeared.

It is the second day since María Teresa stopped going near the toilets. During the breaks she takes up position by the stairs, on the far side of the cloister, making sure that no pupil has stayed in their classroom (this is the latest fad: for some inexplicable reason a few pupils say they do not want to go out at break-time. However, they are not permitted to stay in their classrooms. Going outside for their breaks is compulsory). She is talking to her colleagues a little more. They think she is shy, and are not far wrong. Yes, she is shy, and finds it hard to open up and talk. Now though she spends more time, as was the case a few days earlier, in the assistants' room; this means the conversation flows a little more freely. Of late the assistants have not had all that much to do. As long as the teachers turn up for their lessons, they have quite a lot of spare time. Those assistants who are students use this time for precisely that: to study. Most of them are doing law degrees, a few engineering. María Teresa watches them struggle, ears bright red, to memorise the contents of the weighty tomes they lug around all day. The others chat, almost always about the life of the school, although in recent days the men are all busy talking football (their proud boasting about the Argentinian team even spreads to the women: the World Cup winners of 1978, strengthened by the presence of Ramón Díaz and Diego Maradona, are bound to win again).

María Teresa follows their conversations, although she can rarely think of anything to add. To show she is listening, she nods and smiles. She is hoping Señor Biasutto will not appear in the room. She feels better with other people around, but Señor Biasutto is their supervisor, and so sooner or later he always drops in. In a business-like way, he deals with three or four unresolved issues (taking the requests for punishment to the Head of Discipline, the return of the cinema keys to the janitor's office, his authorization for ordering new white chalks), he has a quiet word with Marcelo, checks the attendance and late-arrivals' sheets. María Teresa has the impression that he is stalking her: that his apparently casual drifting round the assistants' room is in fact no such thing. She thinks he is looking surreptitiously at her. She has no wish to find out if this is so, and bends over the sheet of marks she is completing. Eventually, Señor Biasutto leaves the room.

She tries not to be on her own at break-times, but this goes against the way the assistants work in order to patrol the cloisters as efficiently as possible. Señor Biasutto is always somewhere around. It is quite obvious he wants to approach her, but equally plain that he does not know how to do so. She sometimes sees him staring at her from a distance. At one point in the middle of the third break he heads towards her, but just then she discovers a boy in the seventh or eighth year (it does not matter which) who has the top button of his shirt undone beneath the knot of his blue tie, and so hastily goes over to tell him off. She stands there, making sure the pupil corrects this infraction: he loosens his tie, pulls it down, squeezes the shirt button between two fingers and does it up, then tightens the knot again, straightens it. While all this is going on, Señor Biasutto leaves.

Another day goes by. They all pass slowly now. As is only logical, María Teresa starts using the women's toilet reserved for the assistants. It is smaller and more comfortable, with a towel and soft toilet paper. The door is a proper one, and can be locked, although there are two frosted-glass panels, so there is no complete privacy. Whenever she feels the need, which fortunately is not very often, this is the toilet María Teresa uses, as she did when she first started working at the school. It is not far from the assistants' room: it takes less than a minute to reach it. This is probably the only moment in the entire day that María Teresa is on her own: when she goes to this toilet, and when she comes back. Earlier today she drank two cups of lemon tea almost one after the other, so now she does need to go to the toilet. She hurries there. She takes advantage of the trip to tidy up in front of the mirror, which in this toilet is not streaked. She adjusts the clips she is wearing to keep her hair out of her face. She leaves the toilet to return to the assistants' room. Halfway down the cloister, Señor Biasutto intercepts her. At first it seems as though he is going to walk with her and accompany her, but then he stops and forces her to come to a halt as well.

—Everything all right with you?

—Yes, Señor Biasutto.

He clears his throat.

—Any news? Anything you'd like to tell me?

—No, Señor Biasutto.

He sways oddly from side to side, nodding approvingly.

—Good, very good. I'm really pleased.

He spreads his hands, then suddenly brings them together, as if about to applaud. But he does not do so, or if he does it is in complete silence. It is more a gesture of satisfaction.

—Well then, follow me.

María Teresa nods, and follows him. She does so in a very odd way: she takes the lead, and Señor Biasutto walks behind her. Yet it is true that she is following him, that he is the one choosing where they go, and that she is merely obeying. They reach the end of the cloister, then turn left. They continue towards the tuck shop, but when they reach it, they turn off.

She enters the boys' toilet without taking any great precautions. They are not necessary: Señor Biasutto is with her, and his presence is enough to justify whatever they do. Despite their rapid entry, he does not choose the cubicle at random. He aims for the second from the left, and once inside, María Teresa notices that the broken bolt has already been replaced, good as new, firmly fitted with four new screws (not three, as before). Rough as cigars, Señor Biasutto's fingers slide the bolt across with a clunk that sounds irreversible. María Teresa gazes at him expectantly, as if she does not know. Señor Biasutto avoids meeting her eye.

He is hardly less clumsy than the first time. His hands become knotted, either from haste or anxiety, from his urgent need. He heaves her skirt up so violently that she feels a cold breeze on her legs; he almost tears off her knickers, oblivious to the stretching material. He does nothing at all to make this second time any easier for her. The strict repetition of actions he would like to become a ritual is no compensation either. For María Teresa it is exactly the same: consternation at first, then embarrassment, then terror. She trembles, face pressed against the wall. The only relief she can glean from this painful replay is that this time she knows from the start that Señor Biasutto's thing is not going to play any part in what happens. It is his clumsy hand forcing its way in again, his middle finger groping violently inside her. His strange whimper, the long wait, enduring the pain, the end that has no real end. Señor Biasutto's inane grin, begging her indulgence or bestowing it. The cold in the school toilets.

María Teresa straightens her clothes. Señor Biasutto does not leave the cubicle yet. The afternoon is damp as well as cold, and a thin cloud of steam covers the surface of the toilet tiles. He runs a hand (his left hand) through his stiff, brilliantined hair. Today he seems smaller, stockier, harder to shift. This pause would be inexplicable, but for the bewildered look on his face. Finally he turns round, draws back the bolt, leaves the cubicle. For a moment it seems as though he is going to look at himself in the mirror, not deliberately, but simply because he is going to pass in front of it; in the end he does not do so.

They leave the toilet together. There is no-one in the corridor. They walk for a while side by side until Señor Biasutto comes to a halt. She does the same.

—I want you here on Monday, understood?

María Teresa stares at him.

195

—Here, in the toilet, understood? Searching for those trouble-makers who are breaking the rules.

With this, Señor Biasutto walks off, not caring that she is no longer alongside him. But after a few steps, he slows down and turns back to look at her.

—You understood, didn't you?

María Teresa says nothing.

—You did understand, didn't you?

—Yes, Señor Biasutto.

—Sure?

—Yes, Señor Biasutto.

Señor Biasutto nods.

—Until Monday then.

—Until Monday.

When she reaches the assistants' room where her colleagues are gathered, it seems to her impossible that life is going on as normal. Yet that is what is happening: no-one has noticed a thing, and everything else is following its usual course. The rest of the world, the world of other people, does not change because of what has happened to her: it does not collapse or fall apart, it continues as usual. No ripples, however invisible or unexpected, disturb or upset it. María Teresa is astonished at this proof that things carry on regardless. She is surprised there is not even the slightest unexplained disturbance to everyone else's everyday reality, even though none of them knew anything about what happened to her, and had no way of knowing.

This same feeling returns even more strongly when, a short time later, her work finishes and she leaves the school. In the street, the indolent persistence of the most ordinary things seems to her monstrous. The blue and yellow number 29 bus goes by, heading for La Boca. The corner newspaper kiosk is shut: it only opens in the mornings. The flower seller is listening to the radio by the light of a dangling bulb. People pass by without looking at her, without finding any real reason to be interested in her.

She wants to get home as quickly as possible. On days like these, though, it is as if the difficulties multiply: the queue to buy tokens for the metro is longer than usual, the train takes ages to arrive and depart; at night there are problems and unexpected halts in the tunnels between stations. Only her own rate of walking can be accelerated.

At home, the mother is watching television. The news is showing an interview with Mario Kempes, the hero of the 1978 World Cup. Kempes says he can promise the fans that the colours of Argentina will be raised to the heights once more. Kempes has been playing in Spain for several years, and it is obvious his pronunciation has changed. In the 1978 World Cup he scored six goals, two of them in the final.

María Teresa says hello to the mother, then goes into the bathroom. Contrary to her usual habit, first she soaps her body, and then pours shampoo onto her hand to wash her hair with. She uses roll-on deodorant rather than a spray, because that makes her sneeze, and besides, it does not seem to her very feminine. Sometimes she sprinkles on talcum powder. Today she does.

She dresses casually: gym pants, pyjama jacket, slippers with a furry lining. She sits down to watch television with the mother, but cannot concentrate. The images jump from one thing to another: an earthquake, a race, rain somewhere, a wounded man, a sinking ship, a trench; she can barely understand what she is seeing.

She asks if there is any news from her brother. None at all. He has not written or telephoned. Nothing. She is alarmed.

Curled up in bed later that night, she tries to sleep but finds it impossible. This happens all the time. She tries several new ruses to help her doze off: she has always said her prayers and clutched the rosary in her hands, but now that is not enough. She tries other methods, like imagining her bed is floating in the middle of an icy lake, going over in her mind the names and nicknames of all her friends in the Child Virgin group, fantasizing a journey in which she leaves all her problems behind, letting her mind go blank, pulling the bedclothes over her head, calling on God.

Eventually one or other of these techniques is successful, or perhaps her tiredness finally gets the better of her, and she falls asleep. But in her sleep she dreams. And her cruel dreams wake her up again. This is what happens on the Friday, when she dreams of a tunnel, and on the Saturday, dreaming of a well. And now, precisely now, on Sunday night, as the weekend is reaching its conclusion, she has just had a dream about an ocean; a huge, deep ocean with ten or twelve scattered objects floating in it. These objects are people, and one of those people is her brother. Not all of them have to make the same effort to stay afloat. Her brother, for example, does nothing: he is lying flat on his back as if he had a bed rather than an ocean beneath him, and is floating comfortably. But from the shore a figure she cannot make out very well is holding sheets of paper with lists of names on them. He is reading them out. Although it is a wide-open space, the names are heard crystal-clear. Thanks to some obscure magic, there is a link between a name and a destiny: some drown, others are saved. Still dreaming, or possibly already coming out of it, María Teresa realises that she and her brother both have the same surname. Even though this is obvious, it gives her a jolt.

She wakes up, not sure whether she has cried out or not. Who knows: if she did, she must have disturbed the mother (for some time now she has been a very light sleeper, and for the past few nights has done no more than doze). The night is silent. Her terrifying awakening finds no echo in the rest of the apartment. The curtains are still, the air stagnant, the clock ticks steadily, proclaiming the eternal victory of the present.

María Teresa sits upright in bed, but soon collapses back onto the pillow and under the covers. She goes over the terrifying dream she has just had, in the hope that by remembering the details now she is awake she can repel its distressing effects. She is worried about her brother: about Francisco down in Comodoro Rivadavia. This concern quickly fuses with another. She is petrified to think that in a few hours' time, three or four at most, the alarm clock will go off in this very room, she will be nervous all morning, will not want to eat lunch, and then will leave for school. The next day, which strictly speaking is today, she will have to go to school, as she will on the following days, and she will have to diligently fulfil her duties as a class assistant.

199

She will not be able to get back to sleep until she can separate this truth from the rawness of her nocturnal thoughts. The hours go by. The alarm clock goes off. She is already awake. Awake and thinking what has been constantly on her mind: that she has to go to school and carry out her duties.

The mother meanwhile has switched on the radio.

16

On Monday 14 June 1982, Port Stanley falls. The Argentinian general Mario Benjamín Menéndez, Governor of the islands, signs the surrender in the presence of the British General Jeremy Moore, commander of the victorious forces. This marks the end of the armed conflict, seventy-four days after the Argentinian invasion. In different parts of the islands, the defeated soldiers line up to surrender, piling up their weapons under the watchful eyes of the British troops taking them prisoner. Added together, the number of men lost by both countries in the conflict totals more than nine hundred.

At the National School of Buenos Aires, the pupils are given three days off. There are no classes on Monday, Tuesday, or Wednesday. The assistants tell the pupils this on the staircase up to the front entrance. Once they have done so, they too go home, without entering the locked school building.

On Thursday they resume their activities as normal. By then the school authorities have been completely renewed. There in a new Headmaster. A new Head of Discipline as well. Also a new supervisor of assistants. All of them have been appointed provisionally by the governing body of the University of Buenos Aires to cover the undetermined period that is already being called, both within and outside the school, a period of transition. The previous authorities (the Deputy Headmaster, the Head of Discipline, the assistants' supervisor, and even Mr Vivot) do not reappear to take their leave or to take part in any kind of handover ceremony. Nothing of this kind takes place. On Thursday everyone at the school meets the new staff, who are already in post. Those who preceded them in these positions are simply no longer there. They are no longer there, they no longer come, they will no longer be seen at the school.

Francisco Cornejo returns from Comodoro Rivadavia in an Argentinian Air Force Hercules. It touches down in the early hours of Saturday morning at the El Palomar airbase. The reunion with his family two hours later at the Villa Martelli barracks is restrained but emotional. His mother Hilda and his elder sister María Teresa are waiting for him on the far side of the wooden fence on Avenida San Martín.

Two months after his return, Francisco finds a job in a car factory in Córdoba province. He moves with his mother and sister to a suburb of the provincial capital. The neighbourhood is called Malvinas Argentinas. They live in a typical little villa which has its own modest charm. There is a small back garden, and so they are able to fulfil a long-standing dream and adopt a dog. He's a Labrador, whom they call Tobias.

Monserrat school in the city of Córdoba employs only male assistants. But a manager at the Renault factory with good connections promises to find out if there is a possibility of a job for María Teresa in administration.